CELIBATES

A NOTE ON THE AUTHOR

Pádraig Standún was born near Castlebar County Mayo. He has been a priest for twenty-one years in Connemara and the Aran Islands. He has had four books published in Irish. *Lovers* was published by Poolbeg in 1991.

CELIBATES

PÁDRAIG STANDÚN

POOLBEG

A paperback original
First published 1993 by
Poolbeg Press Ltd
Knocksedan House,
Swords, Co Dublin, Ireland

© Pádraig Standún 1993

Celibates is based on the Author's Irish language novel *Cíocras*,
published by Cló Iar-Chonnachta, 1991

The moral right of the author has been asserted.

A catalogue record for this book is available from the British Library.

ISBN 1 85371 236 1

Cover photograph by Gillian Buckley
Cover design by Pomphrey Associates
Set by Mac Book Limited in Stone 10/13
Printed by Cox & Wyman Limited, Reading, Berks

To Vera and Nadine

"**P**our forth, we beseech thee, O Lord thy grace into our hearts…"

Bríd Sheáin Éamoinn and Sorcha Mhicil were coming to the end of their evening devotions at the shrine built in the Marian year at the end of the eighties. On wet evenings they prayed in the chapel. When the weather was suitable they stood at the outdoor shrine, "The Grotto" as it was known locally.

"May the divine assistance always remain with us…" Bríd's words were suddenly choked by the lump which came in her throat. She had great time for Father Pat, the priest who lay on what was likely to be his deathbed behind the gable against which the grotto was built. She felt as close to him as to any of her own five sons. He had been so good the time Peadar was killed off the motorbike…She sighed aloud as her friend finished the prayers:

"…and may the souls of the faithful departed through the mercy of God rest in peace."

Bríd and Sorcha were friends for more than fifty years, since they started in the national school together. After a while in England in the early fifties they had married two brothers and spent the rest of their lives as next door neighbours. There was hardly a day in which they did not spend some time together. Since the practice of the family rosary in the home had died out they prayed together each evening on their way back from milking their lone cows. The little white plastic milk buckets stood like votive offerings before the shrine as they trimmed the rosary with prayers for themselves, their families and everyone in need.

"How many days is it now?"

"Twenty seven." Bríd tied her scarf tightly before facing into the wind.

"He has a long way to go yet. Didn't some of those young fellows in the North go seventy days and more?"

"They say he has lost two stone weight."

"Mind you, you wouldn't think it to look at him." Sorcha reached for her bucket. "What a pity..."

"I can't see this Pope giving in."

"That fellow thinks that everyone is as tough as himself."

"Father Pat is as strong as any of them." Bríd made a final little bow to the shrine before leaving. "It takes a lot of courage to die for something."

"There ar those that say it is better to live for something."

"Didn't our saviour himself die for something, died for us all..." Bríd seemed to go into a kind of reverie.

"There's a big difference between that and dying for a woman."

"There's more than that to it, Sarah, and you know it. It's not just for himself that Father Pat is doing it."

"I feel for the man as much as the next person."

"It was past time someone took a stand, a stand other than dropping out, as so many other priests did when they wanted to marry." There was no way Pat Barrett could do wrong in Bríd's eyes.

"But didn't he accept all that when he joined up in the first place? It's a bit like one of us trying to get rid of the ould fellows."

"I wouldn't say no to a trade-in." Bríd almost felt guilty for laughing in the circumstances.

"There is no way the church can be for one thing and against another." Sorcha had her own strong views.

"You can't compare the two things at all."

"Well, I think you can." The women took their time. Both liked a good argument. Bríd had no intention of giving in.

"They go in to those colleges at seventeen or eighteen years of age. They come out after being sheltered for seven years. How could they know their own minds? Know whether they need a woman's love or not?"

"Listen, Bríd. I got married at eighteen years of age, without much schooling or any college education. You weren't much older yourself. That doesn't mean we can eye up the first man that walks down the road."

"It's not right. It's not natural to expect anyone to stay single all their lives."

"It's not just priests that stay single, Bríd. How many people stay single to look after an ailing father or mother?"

"That's not natural either."

"If I was young again..." There was a yearning in Sorcha's voice.

"You'd join the nuns."

"I'd have more respect for my freedom. I would't be half as much in a hurry to tie the knot."

They dawdled on in silence for a few moments, a silence broken by Bríd. "Father Pat isn't trying to force every priest in the world to marry, just that they would be allowed do so if they wanted."

"Don't we know well who she is." Sorcha's reply was brief and to the point.

"We have a good idea…" Bríd was slightly flustered, "…in this particular case."

"Only for she left him there would be none of this."

"Well, if you look at it from Teresa's point of view, what choice had she? What future was there for herself and her child?"

"A pity they didn't stay as they were." Sorcha was all for practical solutions. "Everyone knew well what was going on and it didn't knock a stir out of them."

"It was harder on her than on him."

"I can't see how it was, Bríd."

"He had his job." She corrected herself. "He has his job. She had no recognition of any kind, except as his housekeeper."

"Everyone knew well…"

"She wasn't Mrs. Barrett. She didn't have a ring on her finger to prove it."

"Who needs a ring if they care enough about each other?"

"Tell that to the church." Bríd shifted her bucket from one hand to the other.

"Poor little Jennie." Sorcha thought of Teresa's little girl. "This cannot be good for her."

"She is too young to understand."

"You cannot keep anything from a child. They hear, they know that something is wrong. At her age she would have to be asking after the man that was her father, you could say, for three and a half years."

"What can we do, Sorcha, except put them all under the cloak of Our Lady?"

"Isn't it supposed to be from her that he got the whole idea?"

"He had a vision up there at the grotto during the May devotions."

"But how could that be, Bríd?"

"How could Knock be, or Lourdes, or Fatima?" Doubting of that kind was foreign to Bríd.

"What time will you be ready for the dance?" Sorcha thought it time to change the subject.

"I'll be a nice sight at the dance." Despite her self-disparaging remark, the notion cheered up Bríd. "I haven't danced a step in twenty years, except at weddings.

"It's for a good cause." They hurried, realising that there was a lot of preparation to be done.

❧

There was a great night's dancing in the "Three Kings" motel. Darina or Martina McKay had seldom danced as much in one night. Their younger brother, Davoren had spent the night on the dance-floor too, although he was anything but an expert dancer.

"He has it in the head alright, but he hasn't got it in the feet," Darina joked as they watched their brother's big steps, as he tried to waltz with Patricia Farragher, a foot taller, although the same age as Davoren. "We'll have to teach him a few steps."

"What does it matter so long as he is enjoying it? Maybe we weren't too good either at thirteen." Martina always stood up for Davoren. Just two years older, she was always closer to him than to Darina, now almost twenty. It was not that she didn't hero-worship her sister, or at least her lifestyle, her exams all behind her, her weekly paypacket and her flat in Dublin's southside. She couldn't wait for her own schooldays to be over.

"Has he the hots for Patricia?"

"It's a ladder he'll need there."

"You're awful." Darina gave her sister a playful elbow in the ribs as she looked around the hall for her mother. "Is mam gone home?"

"She left after the speeches."

"The collection went well." Martina shook her shoulders, didn't answer. She was ashamed that the local community had to collect money to bring her father home from the United States. At the same time she looked forward greatly to having him home. "I hope he is going to be alright anyway."

"At least he will be able to go into hospital here." Darina repeated a line she must have used a hundred times in the previous couple of weeks. "Every penny he had earned went in a couple of days when he got sick."

"It's a pity he ever went there in the first place." Martina was beginning to feel restless.

"He wasn't to know he would get sick."

"Didn't he have it before, TB, or whatever they call it?"

"That was a long time ago." They watched the dancing for a while. Country and western music was not their scene but they were hardly in a position to object. Anyway it was livened up from time to time with *céilí* music, with "stacks of barley" and "walls of Limerick."

"He's drunk already." Martina looked across disapprovingly to the bar where Darina's boyfriend,

Seamus McAndrew and a couple of his mates drank. Seamus was tall and thin, his hair cut short except for a wisp of a "bob' above his forehead, and a narrow moustache on his upper lip.

"He seems a bit merry alright." Darina gave a little nervous laugh.

"I hope he's not supposed to drive us home. I'm not getting into a car with him in that state."

"You'll be walking so."

"Davoren and myself will walk."

"I think you are only looking for an excuse to walk. There might be more than Davoren going the road with you."

"Not likely."

"What about Colm? Where is he tonight?"

"I wasn't going with Colm. We're just in the same class."

"I heard he used to carry your bag up from the bus."

"That's Davoren's idea of a joke. Anyway, he's grounded."

"Grounded for what?"

"His mother thought he smelled of drink after the disco the last night."

"And did he?"

"How would I know? I think he had a drop of Jonathan Roger's cider."

"Did you have any drop of it yourself?"

"You know my opinion on drink." Darina had no reply to Martina's dig at her boyfriend. They stood in silence watching the dancers. What amazed Darina was what good dancers the oldtimers were when it came to waltzing or *céilí*, though they did tend to make fools of themselves at the modern dances. "What are the discos like now?" she asked her sister.

"They are good when they start, but of course they don't start until the pubs close."

"Things haven't changed much so."

"You would think you were a grandmother the way you're talking. You were going to the discos here yourself until last year."

"Kidstuff." Darina lit herself a cigarette. She felt it gave her a bit of style.

"You would think some of the people had no mouth at all on them."

"You don't smoke?"

"When I get them for nothing."

"You're too young."

"What age were you when you started?" There was no answer to that. She handed Martina her cigarette. The drag ended in a spluttered cough.

"It wasn't me that gave it to you, if mam smells smoke off you."

"Everyone smells of smoke after a night like this. Anyway she'll be asleep when we get back."

"She hasn't a notion, until her little darlings are home safely."

"Speaking of darlings...Your own is coming over." Seamus and his mates came across the floor in the break between dances. "And how is the budding blonde?" said Mickey Carroll, winking at Martina. She did her best to look through him, ignore him.

"Cooool" Mickey dragged out the word.

"The cool clean hero." Macdara Walsh said to no one in particular.

"So cool, she's frozen." Mickey laughed at his own joke.

"Do you want a belt in the bollocks?" Martina's reply was as explosive as it was venomous. She walked across the hall and sat beside Davoren.

"Take it easy lads." Seamus knew that his friends were annoying Darina too.

"We were only joking." Macdara shrugged his shoulders.

"It's time to be motoring," Seamus said. "The bar is closed."

"You're not driving after all that."

"Sure I often drank seven times as much, and there wasn't a bother on me. Anyway the Sergeant is still here, so there'll be no bageen tonight."

"It's the danger of an accident I'm thinking about." Darina took Seamus' hand so that her criticism would not sound too harsh. "They say that it's after closing time most of the accidents happen."

"That's ould fellows that never had to do a driving test."

"Like Tomeen McNicholl." Macdara imitated one of the neighbours, his whole body twisting with every turn of the steering wheel.

"That fellow couldn't drive an ass, never mind a car." Mickey said contemptuously.

"I drive ten times better when I have a good skip on me." Seamus boasted as they headed out of the hall. "The old cortina never goes better than when James here has a full tank on board."

"Well, ye had a good night of it anyway," Mickey said to Darina while Seamus was fumbling with the lock of the car.

"I'd prefer if we didn't have to take anything from anybody. That's not to say we are not grateful, and happy that dad is coming home soon."

"My old fellow wouldn't mind where it came from, so long as he had the price of a pint." Mickey jumped in beside Macdara in the back seat.

"They say it's the last thing Father Pat will ever organise," Macdara said. "They say he's on the last."

"A pity he couldn't be there tonight." Seamus had the car started. Forgetting he had it left in reverse when he backed in before the function, he released the clutch in the hope of taking off with a squelch of tyres on gravel. Instead the car gave a noisy thud against the wall. Nobody spoke as they sat listening to the tinkle of tail-light glass on the ground. The sudden tension was broken by Darina's inability to stop herself giggling. The laughter became contagious as Seamus put the car into first gear and moved off at a snail's pace.

❦

"When I am weak, then I am strong." Paul of Tarsus' line rattled like a mantra in Pat Barrett's head. As he lay against a stack of pillows in the big double bed, he felt weak, very very weak. "Weak-minded" he said out loud to himself, even though he knew that was not the view of him portrayed in the media. That was the heroic picture of a man who had the Pope of Rome himself over a barrel. The image of his holiness bent over a barrel brought a fleeting smile to Barrettt's lips. The surge of pain reminded him of how cracked the same lips had become.

There had been a hint that his hunger-strike had Rome worried. Something indirect his bishop had said about the nuncio. What else would he be talking to the nuncio about? There was no way the Roman authorities would admit, of course that a priesteen out at the edge of the world was a cause of concern to them. A priest putting a hand in his own death, as the

Irish language would put it, the slow, peculiarly Irish death by hunger-strike, a strike against compulsory priestly celibacy.

Pat Barrett was not the first priest to choose death when torn between the love of a woman and the barren rule which forbade clerical marriage in the Roman catholic church. By rope, by tablets or by drowning, the others solved their dilemma. They were buried in clouds of incense, the cause of their self-inflicted violence buried in repetitious ritual, forgotten, except in the hearts of those who loved them.

Barrett had no illusions about how quickly he himself would be forgotten, but for a few long months he would draw attention to this law which left much of his church without a eucharist, the type of attention that only imminent death can draw. One of those months was nearly gone already. No wonder he felt weak...

He took a drink of water from the glass on the little bedside cupboard. His lips were dry and full of sores as was the inside of his mouth. He felt no hunger. That was one of the strangest things, to be dying of hunger and yet feel no pang. The first few days were like that, but the stomach pain died away gradually. One day followed another. Night faded into day and day into night. At first it seemed as if no one was taking any notice. Overnight the communications media took up his story, radio, television, newspapers. They made him a star.

There was a pile of letters about his bed, from people all over the world, people of all races and religions. Of course there were the poison letters. Judas was the kindest name they called him. They prophesied long hot days for him on the flagstones of hell. Then there were the pornographic magazines, perhaps to graphically illustrate what he was missing. The vast majority of those who wrote sympathised with his plight. Many were from clergy in a similar dilemma. But there was no letter from Teresa, no letter or call or visit from the person nearest his heart. He missed her so much, herself and Jennie.

Pat Barrett looked at his watch. Because the blind was drawn now all the time to shield his eyes from the sunlight he tended to mix day with night. It was after two in the morning. They would be going home from the dance about now. That explained the occasional loud laugh or yell outside on the road. He was glad for the McKays. Johnny would soon be home. It had been a tough time for Barbara.

❧

Aisling McAteer was in the same class as Martina McKay, although a year older. They had not met since finishing the Junior Cert in June. They walked home together after the dance, Davoren with them some of the time, twenty metres in front at other times, because he did not care very much for what he considered girltalk. The girls had plenty to talk about. Aisling was working in a hotel in the city for the summer, which left Martina full of envy, as she had to stay home to help her mother and Davoren with the hay. But she was sure things would be different the following year.

"Dad will be at home to do the hay next year, so I'll be able to go working with you in the Lobster Pot."

"If I'm in a hotel it won't be in that one. Work, work, work, scivvying from morning till night."

"I'm sure it's a lot easier than saving hay."

"I'd much prefer it out in the fresh air than working in that shitty place."

"It's waitressing you are?"

"An odd time. That's what the ad in the paper was for. It wasn't a waitress they were looking for but a slave, cleaning floors, washing dishes, even washing out the men's jacks. Ugh…"

"But there's a crowd of you working together. It must be great crack."

Aisling stopped in the middle of the road. "Guess what we found the last day when we were making the beds."

"How would I know?"

"A johnny." Aisling giggled.

"Johnny who?"

"You're so thick. A rubber, you *óinseach*."

"Really!" Martina suddenly remembered that she had not seen her brother for a while. She let a yell at the top of her voice—"DAV…DAVOREN" her unexpected shout knocking a jump out of her companion. That was nothing to the shock both of them got when a throaty voice behind them answered—"I'm here." They roared with laughter and relief when they realised that Davoren had slipped back behind them as they talked animatedly in the darkness.

"You put the heart crossways in me," Martina said when she stopped laughing.

"I don't know which of you is the worst." Aisling gave her friend a playful push. "I got more of a fright from the shout you let looking for your man." Then they all yelled at the tops of their voices, but the element of surprise was gone. Davoren put a hand on each of the girl's backs and pushed them forward.

"We'll never be home with the way the two of ye are walking. Mam will kill us. We're dead, Martina, if we don't get a move on."

"Mam will say nothing to her little pet." Martina knew how to annoy him.

"Not half as much a pet as you are. Hurry up"

"Sure we hadn't a chat for months."

"I don't know what girls and women are always talking about."

"Fellows, of course." Aisling's reply came quickly, and both girls had a fit of the giggles."

"Were ye drinking , or what?" Davoren couldn't see their joke, and with a grunt of desperation he walked on ahead.

"Tell me here," Martina gave Aisling a quick nudge of her elbow. "Is there any fine thing working in that hotel?"

"Why wouldn't there."

"Who is he?"

"It's not a he. It's a she. Me." They were laughing again, like they used to in the school yard, comfortable in each other's company.

"You're so stuck up."

"I wish I was." Aisling gave a shriek of laughter. "Wait until I tell you, do you know who I was out with a few times? You'll never guess...Mickey Carroll."

"I hate him."

"But he's as wild as anything, and he's great crack."

"How is it you weren't with him tonight?"

"The da and the ma were at the dance. They would not approve," she said archly, "but I'll do what I like. They would prefer to see me going out with some pimply teenager."

"He's a lot older than you. He must be twenty or

twenty-one."

"The older the fiddle, the sweeter the tune." Aisling shrieked with wild laughter, as the girls pushed each other here and there across the road in their exuberance. Davoren dropped back to join them, thinking he was missing all the fun. When Martina asked Aisling would she find her a nice fellow from the hotel, he interjected "I'll tell Colm."

"There are more fish in the sea than Colm." Martina decided to get her own back on him. "Wait until dad hears about Patricia longlegs."

"I'll split you if you say anything about her."

"Ye'll have to put higher doors in the house, not to speak of getting a longer bed." Aisling joined in the mocking.

"I'm not going with her. I'm not great with her..."

"But she's very great with you."

"She is not." Davoren shouted, and walked quickly ahead using language Martina never heard from him before, while the girls mocked him with their laughter.

"Did you do it with Colm yet?" Martina pretended she did not know what Aisling was talking about. "Do what?"

"You know well."

"Did you and Mickey?"

"I asked you first."

"Well, if you want to know, no. I have more sense."

"Don't be so oldfashioned."

"It's not oldfashioned. It's newfashioned, with AIDS and everything."

"I think I can hear Sister Damien talking here. Anyway, you're not telling me Colm has AIDS, the poor innocent little crathure."

"Don't be daft. It's just that I don't know I want to

spend my life with him."

"What difference does that make?"

"I think it makes a lot of difference."

"Sure everyone does it."

"A lot brag about doing it because they feel they have to pretend."

"You don't know what you're missing."

"You mean, you and Mickey?"

"You and Mickey what?" Davoren had slowed to let them catch up with him.

"Mickey the dickey." The girls got another fit of giggles.

"I don't know which of you is the daftest. Are ye going home, or are ye waiting here all night? We have a day's work to do tomorrow, the hay in the turlough to be made up."

"I hope it's pissing rain."

"Martina!"

"You know how much I love the hay."

"I wouldn't mind a roll in it myself." Aisling laughed loudly at her own joke.

"Sssssh," said Martina, as they were passing the priest's house on their way back into the village, a mile from the motel.

"Isn't he the daft eejit when you think of it?" Aisling said. "I wouldn't mind but he was a fine thing."

"Do you ever think of anything else?"

"What else is there?" Aisling's infectious laugh rang out on the night air.

❦

Barbara McKay did not go to bed until Martina and Davoren came home, knowing well that she would get no sleep while they were out. As for Darina, what was the point in worrying about her? Living and working in Dublin she could do what she wanted without having her mother looking over her shoulder. But she was a good girl, who came home every chance she got, though Seamus of course was part of the reason for that.

"Off to bed with ye now, and I don't want to hear a gig out of ye before midday." She didn't say anything about them being so late. It was a once-off situation, and she knew how much Martina in particular resented the collection for her father.

"What about the hay?"

"We'll have all evening for that, Davoren. There is a heavy dew promised, so we can let the sun do most of the work for us. We would be only wasting our energy messing about with it before the middle of the day."

"I'm dying with the thirst, mam," Martina said. "Is there any Seven-Up?"

"When did your last servant die? You know where the fridge is. I'm off to bed now. It was a long day. Goodnight, God bless."

"Night..." About an hour later Barbara heard Darina come in. She called into her mother's room— "I'm back, mam." After saying goodnight Barbara turned in the bed, thinking she might get some sleep now at last, but the *céilí* music was still playing in her head, and the thoughts were coming thick, fast and muddled. Her only satisfaction was that Johnny would soon be home.

Cancer was the first thought to cross Barbara's

mind when word first came from the States that her husband was ill. The disease that killed a fifth of the population according to the radio. It would be logical, giving the number of cigarettes he smoked. It was a relief to find it was a recurrence of the tuberculosis he had as a child. At least there was a cure. As an illegal immigrant he had no insurance and the hospital costs there were astronomical.

The locals were great really. As soon as people heard of the illness, fundraising started. People for miles around contributed, but that didn't make it any easier to take. Her biggest fear was that someone would cast it up to the children in the future. Her mind went back to her schooldays, to the time Anne Fahy came into class with a beautiful new dress that had come in a parcel from America. The master had made her stand up for all the classroom to admire, before taking the good out of it with one of the nastiest remarks she had ever heard.

"I remember the time they had a collection for your grandfather, when his old ass died, and now look at the cut of you..."

Looking back now Barbara thought life had been great before Johnny lost the dole. It's not that they didn't row, or that they did anything more than scrape by, but they had enough, their own potatoes and vegetables in the haggard, the mackerel and pollock in the freezer, the eggs free-range. The price of a beast or a lorryload of seaweed paid the bigger bills like the insurance on the old Toyota. They got by comfortably without hunger or poverty.

Then that bitch had come from the Social Welfare, the guager, as she was known locally. Johnny was caught redhanded, Pat Larry's lorry loaded with seaweed standing in the yard as they were having their tea. £25 a week they docked him, the difference between a reasonable living and poverty. Of course he should have appealed it, but he had his pride. He decided to go to the US, to earn enough money to buy a *currach* and engine. He would earn enough from lobster fishing to be able to tell them to stuff their dole.

Barbara applied for the deserted wives' allowance. It was barefaced lying, but it was only lies like that that kept a quarter of the population from abject poverty altogether. This was her way of getting back the money docked from Johnny's dole. The government or the social welfare system were not always as much to blame as the arrogant civil servants that administered their schemes as if the money was coming from their own pockets.

Barbara felt that Johnny had overdone the work in Boston, holding down, not just one job but two. That must have helped to bring on his illness. It seemed like some kind of divine revenge for lying to get the allowance. She felt so strongly about it that she went to confession. She couldn't remember now the example the priest gave, something from the old testament about the people eating consecrated bread because they were hungry. Father Pat said not to worry about it. That didn't ease her conscience completely because he was the kind of a man that made wild statements like saying there was no sin as bad as telling the dole office about your neighbour. What about murder, or adultery?

Still, it cut her to the quick to think of him dying, dying foolishly it seemed in order to try and change the rule of celibacy. A lot of people said he would not go through with it, that he just wanted to see how far could he push things. But he seemed to have almost a mad streak in him. People used to say he was like Christ, and he seemed to have that same desire, almost, for crucifixion. She knew that he was behind the collection for Johnny in a very discreet way. That's the way he was, wouldn't let his left hand know what his right hand was doing when it came to a good turn. When there was something he wanted the world to know, by God he spread the news.

She tossed and turned, eventually letting her mind concentrate on the positive, Johnny's homecoming. She was almost afraid to think of it in case something else went wrong. What would he look like? How weak was he, really? What did it matter as long as he was alive and back with them again? They would put up with a lot in return for that grace. With that thought easing Barbara's mind, sleep stole up on her.

❧

Teresa Carter didn't want to get up. She lay back in bed smoking cigarette after cigarette. Her daughter, Jennie was up and down from the kitchen since morning, spending a while with her grandmother, another while with Teresa. The grate of the fireplace, which hadn't been used since the central heating was installed was Jennie's cot for her doll. She busied herself changing her "baby" and putting it to bed.

It was the first morning since they left that Jennie had not mentioned Pat. She must have noticed the previous day how mention of his name brought tears to her mother's eyes. She had put her little arms around Teresa and given her a hug. They missed the *naíscoil*, the playschool Jennie had gone to in the west.

It was surprising the amount of Irish Jennie had picked up in a short time. Teresa herself had little enough of it, but Pat was fluent. Pat, Pat...Could she think of anything that Pat was not part of?

He must have twenty eight or twenty nine days done now, she thought. There was hardly a day she did not reach for pen and paper to write to him. She put them aside again. That side of her life was over. Instinctively she knew that it would not be over until he... Yes, say it, until he died. His life or death were as much in his own hands as they were in the hands of the bishop or the Pope.

The hunger-strike put her under enormous pressure and stress. He would not be doing it if she had not left him. He would give it up if she were to go back. He hadn't said that, but she knew. He hadn't said anything. He had taken her so seriously when she had said she didn't want any contact, that she wanted to put that part of her life behind her. She would give anything to see him again. She would and she wouldn't. "O, Christ, but it's tough." The pain of loneliness, the sadness inside her was physical.

They would have been better to have finished up consumed in bitterness and rancour like so many couples that could not put up with each other any more. They were civilised, too civilised by half. She couldn't live with him and she was finding it very hard to live without him. He had often said that the hunger-strike was the only way to pressurise the church authorities. But why was it he who had to do it? Why could he not leave and marry as many of his colleagues had done? Pat Barrett had to be different. He had to take the whole burden on himself.

That was really why she had left him, because he

had a choice between marrying her and remaining as a priest in the church. He had chosen his sterile church. He would argue that the church shouldn't present its clergy with such a dilemma. He would cite the protestant churches. He had all the arguments, all the logic to support his case. But it was her life too. She wanted an ordinary life, a marriage, children, Pat's children.

Strange how often she forget that Jennie was not Pat's child. She hardly ever thought of the real father, Emmet. She had probably never known him that well, although she was cracked about him at the time. Summer love. A holiday fling. Even now he probably didn't realise he was a father. Despite all his protestations of undying love he had never even written after going back that September. That was the year she had worked in the Gaeltacht hotel, the year of her leaving cert, life mapped out safely and sensibly before her. She had even qualified for university when she found out that she was pregnant.

A pity she hadn't gone on anyway, carried her pregnant belly around the campus, breastfed her way through First Arts. She would be qualified now. A pity. A pity...Was there anything in life but missed opportunity? But she would do it now. Her mother would mind Jennie, Monday to Friday. She would qualify. By Jesus she would qualify or die in the attempt, for her own, for Jennie's sake. She was finished with men, with love, with romance. What did it bring except heartache?

Where would she be without Jennie? She was her life, her heartbeat, her reason, her only reason to live. Looking at her now with her doll would raise even the heaviest heart, and Teresa felt her own was certainly one of them. She knew she should shake herself, jump out of the bed, do something, anything. She knew... She knew it all, but she couldn't do anything, she thought, while Pat was the way he was. It was as if he had her under a spell, some sort of *geasa* like the old fianna had. She was strikebound as long as he was on hunger-strike.

If Emmet knew about Jennie. He might even contribute to the upkeep of his child. But he might make an attempt to get custody. It was a very small chance, but even that much she would not give to anyone. Jennie was her life. She would die without her. But would manage without any man.

Wasn't it she that was wild and free that summer too? She was paying for it since. Who would believe it was only four years ago? A whole lifetime seemed to have passed. Four years. She could be qualified now, and not a thing for it, but heartache... But that was not true either. She had a healthy, goodlooking daughter, her father's wide forehead, her mother's auburn hair.

It was from her father the good looks came, Teresa thought as she watched Jennie change her doll's nappy for the third time. Teaching an Irish course had brought Emmet west, teaching by day, drinking in the Óstán by night. A party on the beach every night after closing time. Music, bonfire, six-packs, *poitín*. Swimming nude at two or three o'clock in the morning. A wonder no one had been drowned.

It was in the sea that Emmet had kissed her the first time, after the two of them had swum a race out to the lobster storage box. Having being reared half a mile from a Burren beach Teresa was a good swimmer. She beat Emmet by thirty yards. Holding onto the buoy that marked the storage box, she waited for him to arrive. He was out of breath. Little wonder with the amount he smoked and drank. Emmet hung on to the rope beside her until he got his breath back.

"Thanks," he had said. "Thanks very much."

"For what?"

"For waiting for me. I could have drowned going back if you hadn't waited. I took on a lot more than I'm able for." It was then that he kissed her. It wasn't her first kiss. There had been many a kiss and a grope at the youth club, but this seemed special. Because Emmet seemed special. Feelings went through her that she hadn't experienced before. It was strange to feel wet down there and you up to your neck in water. Emmet did not touch her as they swam back slowly together, or at any time that night. But she knew it was only a matter of time.

"We were playing with the lobsters," Emmet explained their delay when they reached the beach. "*Crúbáil*," someone had said. "There's always pawing where you have lobsters."

"*Crúbáil* it would be if you were involved," Emmet had said, and the night almost ended in a row.

The following evening they were together in her bed in the staff quarters of the hotel. How did either of them manage a day's work from then on? They were in each other's arms any time they were free. They never seemed to sleep for more than a couple of hours at a time. One or other of them would wake, and the *crúbáil* would start. That word remained with them. It was not just in the staff bedroom either, but on the beach, in the car, anywhere. There was no talk of care or of condom. They were in love.

Although she began to wonder about him as the Autumn slipped on, it did not occur to her that she had missed her period. She was never much good at keeping dates. It had never mattered before. When she began to be sick in the mornings, a girl who shared a flat with her asked could she be pregnant. It was not that she hadn't known the facts of life, as they called them. Her head had been turned. In some way she felt everything would be alright because they loved each other. They would marry or something. Love would find a way.

She tried to get in touch with Emmet. He had taken a leave of absence from his teaching job. She thought she remembered him saying that. His former flatmate thought that he was in the United States, but it might have been Australia. Teresa gave up at that stage.

The girl in the flat said she knew of a priest who was very understanding. She discussed everything from abortion to adoption with him. He was non-judgemental, kind. When he said she could stay in his house during the pregnancy, that she wouldn't be the first, she had accepted the offer. At that stage she felt she couldn't face her mother. How wrong she had been about that, as she was to find out later.

Pat Barrett told her he was trying to help undo some of the damage done by priests over the years, priests who had "read" girls who were single and pregnant from the altar. The biggest difference between herself and the other girls who had stayed with Pat was that she had stayed on after the birth of her baby. The early months were a blur of feeding, nappies, waking during the night. Then, almost suddenly it seemed that Jennie had grown, was walking, talking, looking on Pat as her "dada." It was hard to leave then, when both mother and daughter were in love with him.

Although the way of life suited both of them at

that stage, Teresa felt now that she had known from the beginning that it would not work longterm. She did not want to be seen as a housekeeper when she was a wife in all but name. She wanted to stand beside him, help with his work, be invited to weddings and christenings as his wife. Was she asking too much? What woman would accept less? Maybe she hadn't loved him enough, loved him too much? How was she to know? She should really have left much sooner, before it became too difficult.

The break seemed to affect him more than her. He felt she had put a gun to his head, and in a way she had. He was looking for too much, to have things both ways, every way. In some ways he was an idealist to the marrow. A priest to the marrow too. He saw no reason why he could not have the moon and sun as well. But there was a reason. A big reason. The laws and traditions of his own church for one thing. He had tried to have everything but was left with nothing. Left without life itself it seemed before very long.

ᵴ

Tuesday. A wet day. Signing-on day, and for some, a drink day. Neddy John Tom was telling of his adventures during the second world war. Everybody knew that potato picking in Scotland was as near as Neddy had got to the action. But it would be a shame to contradict him. His fiction was better than fact any day.

"I was within a hundred yards of Adolf the same day. Him inspecting his troops as they goose-stepped up and down in front of him. We were there in the trenches, water up to our waists, holding up our rifles to keep the powder from getting wet, rats as big as month old bonhams hopping around us." Neddy had seen a lot of films about a lot of wars and tended to run them together.

"Hop up the ladder, Irish," says the captain. "Bart was his name, or Bert...It doesn't matter now. We had our own names for him, though old Bart wasn't the worst. There was no harm in him, a decent man, as Englishmen go. A right Long John Silver, with one leg, and a Victoria Cross from the first war. A brave man. A tough man. A man who wouldn't send his soldiers where he wouldn't go himself."

"And you went up on the ladder." Dara Nóra winked at the others.

"Sure Neddy would go up on a whin bush." Tomeen McNicholl showed a lot of toothless gum as he laughed at his own joke.

"Ah...Fuck ye."

"Take plenty of no notice, Neddy. Tell your story." Dara Nóra sounded so sincere that it might be forgotten that it was himself made the first interruption. Neddy stood looking into his pint, as if trying to make up his mind whether to sulk or not.

"Go on, Neddy," Tomeen said. "I didn't mean anything."

"Double fuck you," was Neddy's reply, but he decided to go on when he noticed Tomeen ordering a pint for him.

"'Be careful Irish,' says one of the Tommies behind me, as I edged my way up the ladder. I could hear Bart saying to the lads—'if there's anyone who'll give it to the bastard between the eyes, it's Irish.' 'Sssssssh,' I gave them a sign to be quiet, when they started to shout—'Good on you, Pat.' I didn't want them to frighten the old fox, as it were. I climbed up slowly, glad to be out of the water. I didn't even have my helmet on, a bit of muck on my forehead, so the huns wouldn't see anything moving. 'Don't shoot,' Bert said, 'until you see the whites of his eyes.' I'll never forget his words, 'the whites of his eyes.' I peeped up. The Führer...The fucker was only from here to the school away from me. I straightened up my trusty 303 and got him in the sights."

"A sight for sore eyes." Tomeen was beginning to be caught up in the story, despite its improbability, impossibility.

"'Let 'im ave it, Irish!' Bart says, 'but wait until you see the whites of his eyes.' 'Impossible, Bart,' I say, unless he has an eye in the hole of his arse. The bastard has his back turned.'"

"Fair fuckin' play to you," said Tomeen, "and what did Bart say?"

"Do you know what Bart said?" Neddy had a go at an English accent. "'A Britisher never shot a man in the arse. It's not on that we built our empire but on fair play and good sport'"

"If they didn't shoot them in the arse, they shot them in the back." Tomeen was getting excited. "What about the Black and Tans?"

"Don't worry, Tomeen. I told him the history of Ireland from top to bottom, from stem to stern, as we used to say in the navy, from beginning to end..."

"But we're not near the end yet." The drop was rising in Tomeen's head "There will be no end to it until the last Englishman is turfed out of Ireland, until Ireland is free, and united."

"And gaelic." Dara enjoyed watching the bicycle-clip bachelor revolutionary in full flow.

"And gaelic. You took the word out of my mouth, Dara."

They moved towards the fire. The crowd that were in the bar earlier had evaporated, cows to milk, cattle to feed before nightfall.

"Isn't it fierce the hurry that does be on some of them, come evening."

"It's alright for you, Neddy, that has no wife or child, no dog or cat"

"I don't see any hurry on yourself, big and all as your family is, Dara."

"They are big enough to do all the jobs themselves now." Dara boasted.

"It's better than any riches."

"What is, Neddy?"

"The full of the house of children to do the work, a big dole to drink, and a wife to ride when you go home." Tomeen didn't like that kind of talk. It was time to change the subject.

"The McKays had a good night of it. I hear that Johnny will be home soon."

"I'm glad for them. They had a hard year." Dara didn't want to say much. His daughter, Aisling was a friend of young Martina. Tomeen tried another tack:

"Isn't it sad about Father Pat."

"It is and it isn't." Neddy supped his pint. "Sure it's himself that decided to do it."

"He'll give it up." Dara sounded sure of himself. "He'll give it up when he finds out how far they are prepared to go. He's a cute hoor, Father Pat, a cute Mayo hoor, and they don't come much cuter than that."

"I don't know about that." Neddy shook his head. "Father Pat is like my old ass. There's no reverse in him. It's a divil when you're on the bog. No going back. You always have to bring him around in a circle."

"Isn't it a shame," said Bartley, the publican who had stepped out of the kitchen to check on their pints, "that's it's here it had to happen."

❧

They walked in the wood to the south of the road between Cong and Clonbur. A beautiful sunny day. Jennie trotted on before them, Teresa and himself telling her to stay away from the water's edge. They climbed up the hill to the limestone monument one of the Guinness family had built in memory of his wife. They sat on the steps. Pat tried to kiss Teresa, but her lips seemed to fade away. Although she was sitting beside him, Teresa was in slow flight out over the Corrib, Jennie hanging onto her neck. "Mind, the child will fall," he shouted after her. His shout awoke him, lying in a cold sweat.

He had been having strange dreams for some time. "I wouldn't mind if I had been drinking red wine, or *poitín*," he said to himself aloud, "but not having drunk anything but water for a month." The jug of water at his bedside had been topped up while he slept. Neighbours came in from time to time to help. They might not agree with what he was doing, but they would see that at least he was comfortable. Not that there was much to do except fill the jug, and change the bed from time to time. Still the women cleaned and scrubbed, even painted. "Getting ready for the wake," he thought, then chided himself for his sarcasm.

He hardly left the bed any more. They had even set up a chair type portable toilet beside his bed, the kind he used to see when in the homes of the old and sick. They seemed to be taking him seriously anyway. "The die is cast," he said aloud. "The die is cast." He had put his hand to the plough. There was no going back. He thought of Christ's statement that the person who puts his hand to the plough and turns back is not fit for the kingdom of heaven, but that was in another context. The same Jesus didn't face death without his own doubt, without sweating blood, without that desperate cry of loneliness and despair,—"My God, my God, why have you forsaken me?"

The long Irish experience of hunger-strike gave him a good idea of what to expect. From the books written about Terence McSwiney in the early twenties to Bobby Sands and his companions in the early eighties there was plenty of well documented information. The various senses weakened, the eyes gradually lost their sight, the ears their hearing…The whole body, the brain gradually gave way—maybe that was the cause of the strange dreams. "But I don't think so," he said to himself. "My mind feels clearer, more uncluttered than ever." And then a little laugh— "If it is, what has me talking to myself out loud?"

Pat Barrett wondered, not for the first time, had he had a nervous breakdown, was his hunger-strike a cry for the help he did not realise he needed. He had been devastated when Teresa and Jennie left and remembered most of all how he used wander from room to room in the silent presbytery crying aloud, his body racked by uncontrollable sobs. He would find something from among Jennie's toys, a lost piece of lego, maybe, and give vent to the hurt he felt inside in screeches of desperation and despair.

There had been hope some time previously that the church would take an honest look at the damage compulsory clerical celibacy caused its own organisation. The bishop of Galway, Éamonn Casey had resigned, admitted to being the father of a seventeen year old in Connecticut. Catholics generally reacted with great tolerance and understanding, to the surprise, and, it seemed, disappointment of many in the news media. For a while it seemed that there might be a chink in the hierarchical armour, but ranks had closed, hatches were battened down on the bark of Peter. The mailed fist began to replace the ham fist as a winnowing process started, to root out priests who might be in danger of compromising the church by failure to live up to their vows.

Looking back now on what had to a great extent been a month's rest, the longest time he had spent in bed in his life, Pat Barrett wondered if he had literally been out of his mind when he had felt Mary, the mother of Jesus had given him a message as he knelt at her shrine during the May devotions. The idea that he should go on a hunger-strike to force the Pope to change his mind on the subject of celibacy had come to him like a bolt from the blue. He had agonised and meditated, done everything except discuss it with anyone. It had been as if he had found a treasure and wanted to keep it for himself. He had needed martyrdom, an easy escape from painful reality, having his cake and eating it, killing himself for a good cause. It had all seemed so logical, so right, at the time.

The hardest part of all was hurting the people you loved most. He could still see his mother's face the last time that she came to visit. She seemed to have aged overnight. Over the years he had never noticed her get older. She seemed like the same mother all the time. Now she looked her seventy years, a look of love mixed with failure to understand in her eyes. "Why are you doing this to me?"—a biblical echo. Was it not often said that it is a hard life for mothers? For the mother of God even—"Who is my mother? Who are my brothers?" echoed down the centuries, the millenia. Must have hurt Mary like hell. Yes it is hard especially on mothers that bring idealists into the world.

There was something, maybe an Irish thing, about priests' mothers. Because their sons did not, could not marry, the priest in some way remained a child always to his mother. He wished that she had died before him. But when someone is driven, drawn to a great deed, can anyone be let stand in the way? Was anything worth that much? One minute he was sure it was, the next he was in serious doubt. He did not want to die. Nobody else, from the Pope down wanted him to die. That was his strength, really, and his weakness. He could give up the strike at any time. The authorities knew that too, and bided their time. No authority liked compromise, forced compromise, especially.

Thomas Doherty, his bishop, was doing his best to find a way out of the dilemma. A gentle man, a cute man, a man who admitted privately that he saw little sense in compulsory clerical celibacy in this day and age. There was no danger though that he would hang such colours to any public mast. The chief characteristics of bishops appointed in the previous ten years were safety, conservatism, cuteness, above all cuteness. Thomas Doherty had what the football fraternity would describe as a safe pair of hands. He would do nothing the Pope might disapprove of. He was too good a church politician for that. But if a solution was to be found, it was he who would find it.

There was another question a man drawing death to himself had to face up to, the judgement of God. Pat Barrett felt that he was following his conscience, even if he was going against the wishes of the church authorities. Was it conscience or his own self-made ideology he was following? Nothing seemed clear any more. He drifted into sleep again, or was it just a daydream?

There was a beautiful young girl, browneyed and sallow with dark dark hair drawing water from a well. She was barefoot and wearing a rough homespun dress which looked something like an old flourbag with holes for the arms and legs. He knew it was the virgin Mary. It seemed natural that he should be on that Bethlehem road, more a path really. "A great pair of legs," he thought, even though he knew he should be thinking of highminded heavenly things. She smiled, a knowing, enigmatic, Mona Lisa kind of smile. Then she shook her head, gently, disapprovingly.

ɤ

Cóilín a' Phortaigh was upset. Snatches of overheard conversation told him that the priest was dying of hunger. Cóilín couldn't understand that at all. He had never heard of a priest that was poor, never mind hungry. If it went to that, they had exactly the opposite reputation of being *santach*, greedy. But then Father Pat was different from any other priest he had known.

Cóilín lived in a little shack on a small rocky peninsula, an island really, except that you could walk out to it at low tide. It was a mile to the nearest house, and Cóilín was considered strange, an *éan corr* or odd bird. He was reputed to be rotten with money, though he lived a life of abject poverty. It came as a major surprise to Cóilín when his dole was stopped and he was told in the post office to apply for the pension.

"Pension? What would I be doing with a pension? Sure I'm not half pension age."

His nearest neighbour, Neddy John Tom told him to go to the priest, that he would sort it out for him. Pat Barrett had no difficulty in proving from the baptismal record that Cóilín was indeed sixty six years old. The difficulty was in convincing Cóilín, who could neither read or write, and thought the whole affair was some kind of government conspiracy, because the wrong crowd were in power. He had always voted for what sounded to the priest like "The Flera" but was of course, Éamon de Valera. He solved the problem to everyone's satisfaction by declaring that the great man had left Cóilín a special pension, as he had been one of his staunchest supporters.

A man of Cóilín's loyalty could not reject such an offer, even if it came long before it was due. In fact, when de Valera retired from the presidency party activists had found it hard to persuade Cóilín that he could no longer vote for his hero. That one was solved by convincing him that it was a child of the long fellow that was running for election in his place, which explained the name "Child-ers."

A friendship developed between Cóilín and the priest while Pat Barrett was trying to sort out the pension problem. They would go to the pub together about once a month. Cóilín had been barred in the past, and felt he would not be allowed in on his own. Barrett would leave him at the edge of the island afterwards, or Cóilín would stay in his house if there was a high tide, and he could not get back home. It upset Cóilín to hear his friend might be hungry. He put eggs and potatoes in a bag and set out for the village.

He was too shy to knock on the door when he reached the presbytery. He heard no noise inside, but noted that the car was in the shed. He looked in the church but the priest was not there either. Cóilín sat on the doorstep, and waited. He sang himself a little song to keep himself company. When there was no sign of the priest, he stretched out on the stone step at the front door, and dozed.

"Oh, Jesus Christ..." Bríd Sheáin Éamoinn got the fright of her life when she arrived in the dusk of the evening to leave fresh water for the priest. Cóilín slowly straightened himself.

"You're after giving me an awful fright, Cóilín." He rose to his feet, and removed his cap in respect. "How are you yourself, maam, yourself and the man of the house?"

"The man of this house?" Bríd beckoned towards the door, "or my own man?"

"The two of them. I hear that this man inside is hungry."

"Why didn't you walk in to see him? The key is in the door."

"I wouldn't like just to walk in."

"Isn't he your best mate?"

"He's a priest all the same. I wouldn't like to be bothering him." He held out his old dirty canvas bag. "Would you mind giving him this?"

"What is it?"

"A few eggs and potatoes. I wouldn't like to think

of the poor man going hungry."

"Come on in and have a chat with him." Bríd held open the door, and Cóilín followed her in. Pat Barrett gave him a big welcome and asked Bríd to get him a glass of whiskey. She put him sitting in the big armchair in the corner, and left the men together when she had filled up the jug of water.

"I brought you a *glaicín* of potatoes and a few eggs." Cóilín put down the bag beside his chair. The priest gave the old Irish thanks and blessing "May you be seven times better off this time next year."

"I don't be talking to that many, but I heard you didn't have very much to eat. Neddy John Tom was telling me it's dying with the hunger you are."

"That'd be Neddy's story alright. It's not that I'm wanting for anything, Cóilín, it's a fast more than anything, a kind of fast and abstinence."

"I didn't think there was any kind of a lent at this time of the year. It's mostly in Spring it used to be, but sure things are changing all the time"

"This is a kind of a lent I took on myself." He didn't know how to go about explaining it to Cóilín.

"My mother, God rest her used to say that the saints were always fasting."

"Half the world is fasting, Cóilín, for the want of something to eat. But whatever about the hunger, don't be thirsty anyway. Have another drop of that American whiskey."

"It's mighty stuff that American whiskey, a grand sweet taste to it."

❦

Johnny McKay sat in the big jet at Boston airport,

waiting for take off. Information was flashed on the big screen in front about safety belts, lifejackets beneath the seats, escape hatches in the event of an accident. Hostesses in neat green uniforms mimed the various ways to follow the screen instructions. Johnny's mind was far from what was being shown.

He was so delighted to be going home. He had not realised the extent to which he loved Barbara and the children until he was away from them. "I can't wait..." was a phrase he had heard so often as his family were growing up. He felt like a child now—"I can't wait to get home." Things were not too bad until he had become ill. The work kept him occupied. Since then it had been hell, bored out of his mind, nothing to do, not able to do anything anyway, one television channel worse than the next. A fish out of water.

Even if you were unemployed at home or off sick, you could walk out to look at the cattle, or along the coast looking for wrack, stand talking to a neighbour. But to be sick in a city during the heat of summer. Whoever said hell was hot knew what they were talking about. Another few minutes and the plane would be taking off, the end of the bad dream that was his stint overseas.

The streets of Boston were not paved with gold. You earned any dollar you got. The work itself was not the worst, but the continuous travel, an hour and a half to the workplace, the same back, half an hour to the night job. Travel, work, travel, work, sleep. Talk about a treadmill. It was not too bad for the young single people. They could go to dances, pubs, go courting. But a married man far from home, trying to save money...

As lonesome as the life was, it was not too bad as

long as he was earning, saving money, knowing that he would be home before the next Christmas. All he wanted was to go through the purgatory of the work, to earn the dollars, to buy the *currach* and engine, to pass on the skills of lobster fishing to Davoren.

It was not that he would expect Davoren to spend his life fishing, but it was no burden to anyone to have an extra skill or trade. Johnny felt that parents in Ireland had not enough respect for their own skills, skills on land and on sea, farm and kitchen, bog and shore, skills that had been handed on for so long that they had almost become innate. Too much attention was paid, he felt to book education. But the other skills were education too, and why deprive young people of them.

The way life was going you would not know when such skills would be needed. A young generation was growing up that could not set or dig potatoes not to speak of anything more complicated. In the event of a natural or manmade disaster, the younger generation would not have the basic skills even of growth or harvesting. The young people were not to blame for this, but the adults who thought office work more important than spadework. Why not have both? Insofar as they could he and Barbara had tried to rear their children with a broad range of skills.

The noise of the jet engines shook Johnny out of his daydream. He felt nervous while the plane was rising but forgot about it after that. He was on his way home.

❧

Teresa Carter waited until it was exactly one o' clock

before she left the bed. Then, like an astronaut getting ready for takeoff, she counted down, "Five, four, three, two, one, blastoff." She tossed aside the duvet and jumped out onto the floor. She pulled on the clothes she had worn for a couple of days. She didn't mind how she looked any more.

"Where are you going?" her mother asked as she emerged uncombed from the bathroom a couple of minutes later.

"Out."

"Without a breakfast?"

"It's dinnertime now, or lunchtime, as they say in the better circles."

"Eat something anyway, breakfast, dinner or tea. You're not eating anything. You'll soon..." Mary Carter hesitated.

"Go on. Say it... You'll soon be as bad as your man that's on hunger-strike."

"Teresa..."

"Just leave me be, mam."

"At least you might take Jennie with you. The poor child looks lost, doesn't know whether it's coming or going you are." Teresa shrugged her shoulders, but when she looked at Jennie her heart softened. She stretched out a hand, and couldn't help smiling when she saw how Jennie's eyes lit up. With a teddybear almost as big as herself under one arm she took Teresa's hand. They went out the back door and out towards the sea. The last thing Teresa wanted was to meet someone, anyone. She was glad that the normally talkative Jennie was quiet, although she twisted, turned, skipped and walked while still holding on to her mother's hand.

"I'll have to pull myself together, for her sake,"

Teresa said to herself. "She would probably be full of chitchat now if I had not been ignoring her for so long." Out loud she said "Talking to me must be like talking to the wall."

"Talking to the wall." Jennie was amused with the idea. "Hello wall," she said to the neatly built limestone that was twice her height. Teresa was feeling better already. She swept Jennie up into her arms, hugged, kissed and carried her along in her arms. It was a beautiful day, the sun reflecting brightly off the grey rock and shimmering out on the sea.

"I'm hot," Jennie said. Her mother helped her to get off her jumper, and took to opportunity to remove her own loose cardigan. She left both garments on the wall, knowing that they would be coming back the same way. There was no other way, as the boreen was a cul de sac petering out on the crag near the little beach where Teresa and her brothers and sisters had learned to swim. Some long forgotten county council scheme had run out of money and the road had stopped forever. "The road to God knows where," Teresa thought.

"Will you come for a swim with me, Jennie?"

"Can teddy come too?"

"Teddy can sunbathe on the beach while we are in the water. We would never have him dry by bedtime if he went into the water, and I don't think you would like going to bed without your boyfriend."

"He's not my boyfriend. He's my girl boyfriend."

"Either way I think it's better not to wet him, her...it."

"Silly mammy." Jenny cocked her head sideways. "You didn't bring togs."

"We don't need togs down here. It's our own

private beach. We'll be all on our ownio. I hope."
Teresa's afterthought was Tomeen McNicholl, who
was supposed to be a bit of a peeping Tom. Then she
remembered Tomeen was part of the other life, life in
the west. The beach was as out of the way as you could
get, a short stretch of sand between the limestone
cliffs. They had great fun in the water, splashing about
and throwing water at each other. Teresa did not
actually swim herself, afraid to let Jennie out of her
sight even for a moment. Too many accidents
happened in that kind of weather. The little girl had
her first real swimming lesson, and played contentedly
on the beach, while her mother stretched out on the
hot sand beside her.

Teresa felt as if a black cloud had lifted from her
mind. It might be the fresh air, the ozone, the salt
water that did it. That didn't matter. The great weight
had lifted, temporarily, at least. She knew they would
be alright, Jennie and herself. On their ownio, maybe,
but facing up to a new life. When she thought of Pat
it was without anger, bitterness, even sadness. Just
love, she thought.

As she expected, swimming in the nude was worse
in her mother's eyes than swimming out of sight or
hearing of others, in case a person got into difficulty.
Teresa sensed that while the older woman made
fussing noises about what would the neighbours think,
she was happy to find her in better form. "I'll get the
dinner today, mam," she offered.

"Don't poison us whatever you do." They smiled
at each other.

❦

They discussed the usual items at the monthly meeting of the community council, potholes, the social employment scheme, houses for young couples. Satisfaction was expressed at the success of the collection for Johnny McKay. It seemed to Sorcha Mhicil that they were just going through the motions. She put the question that she was sure was upmost in every mind. "Can we do anything to end Father Pat's hunger-strike? Nobody wants to see him dying."

"Nobody except himself." Pádraig McAteer, the eldest of Dara Nóra's family replied quickly. A secondary schoolteacher in the community college, he was one of the first fruits locally of the free education scheme introduced in the late sixties. "You can't go anywhere without people asking who is the *amadán* that's trying to do away with himself."

"Father Pat is no *amadán*." Sorcha sprang to the priest's defence. "It's his life. He can do what he likes with it."

"That's the same as saying a woman can have an abortion—she can do what she likes with her own body."

"It's not the same thing at all, Pádraig. We all know that abortion is murder."

"Isn't this murder too, self-murder."

"Could we stick to the point, please?" Sean Donlon, the chairman and principal of the college said. "Can we do something practical, negotiate an arrangement with the bishop, maybe, do something to get him, to get both of them off the hook."

"If he won't listen to Pope or bishop, he's hardly likely to listen to us." Pádraig said.

"We are his parishioners all the same." Bríd Sheán Éamoinn spoke for the first time. "You would expect a priest to pay heed to his parishioners."

"That'll be the day." The chairman ignored Pádraig's interjection, and spoke directly to Bríd and Sorcha. "Would the two of you speak to him? Don't you be in and out looking after the house?"

"I would be willing," Bríd answered, "to tell him the views of the community council, but I'm personally not going to ask him to give up. I think he's right."

"There's no point in asking someone who agrees with the hunger-strike to ask him go give it up." Pádraig said. "Who am I to say? Maybe you all agree with him." He stood up, ready to leave. The chairman tried to hold the meeting together. "Negotiating, talking with him is all I'm talking about. It shouldn't matter if the person bringing the message agrees or disagrees."

"Something needs to be done before he's too far gone to understand." Sorcha said.

"He had reached that point the day he started." Pádraig was still standing up. "As far as I'm concerned he has been out of his mind for a long time."

"A lot agrees with him too," Bríd insisted. "I heard a nun saying on the radio that women should go on hunger-strike too, for the right to be ordained. It's the only thing the holy father will listen to."

"But will he?" Sean Donlon, the chairman said quietly. "He'll split the church down the middle, if he gives in to what is essentially blackmail."

"Now you're talking." Pádraig sat down. "That's what I've been trying to say all along."

It was after midnight when they decided their best course of action was to ask the bishop to intervene urgently again in the matter.

❦

"I think it was expecting a coffin you were." Johnny McKay joked as he left the airport terminal, his family around him, Davoren pulling the trolley with his two suitcases.

"To tell you the truth," Barbara said, "I was ready for anything, except a coffin, of course. It would not have surprised me if you had to be brought out to the car on a wheelchair."

"I'm fine, a bit weak. The doctor beyond gave me a ticket for the hospital here."

"We have the hay saved." Davoren cut in on his parents' conversation.

"Well done the lot of ye. Ye didn't need me back at all."

"We did, we did," came the chorus.

"We're never letting you out of sight again." Martina was loosening the twine that held the door of the boot of the old Toyota estate.

"Old Betsy is still alive anyway." Johnny laughed as he stood looking at the rusty old car, parked between a state of the art BMW and a Range Rover.

"I wish we had one of them." Davoren looked in the window of the BMW, but jumped back immediately when he saw a man lying in the back seat, asleep. The others laughed at the fright he got.

"See is he alive or dead," Darina joked. "It might be a spy. They are always getting knocked off at airports."

"Look yourself." Davoren had seen enough.

"If Betsy brings us home OK, we'll forgive her everything," Barbara said. "Do you want to drive?"

"The doctor said not to stress myself. I think driving around an airport would come into the category of stress." Johnny sat into the left front seat, after letting in the children. Both side doors at the back were jammed with rust from living so near the sea. As they pulled out of Shannon, Davoren asked would there be enough money left out of the collection to get a new car.

"We're ashamed enough as we are, without getting a new car." Martina's reply hung in the air, nobody wanting to comment for fear of a row. Davoren tried to break the tension.

"I'm not talking about a completely new car, but a car without any rust on it."

"Later, love," his mother said. "We don't want to set tongues wagging."

"When I have money I'm going to pay back every penny." There was a harsh edge to Martina's tongue. "They'll have nothing to talk about then."

"People gave the money from their hearts," Barbara said, "and they wouldn't want anything back. It's just that it would look silly and ungrateful if we started throwing money around."

"Have we not talked enough about that?" The topic made Darina uncomfortable. "Isn't the main thing that Dad is back safe and sound."

"I'm delighted you were able to get off work to join the rest of them." Johnny sat sideways in the front seat, so that he would be able to see his children better as he talked to them."

"I kept all my holidays until now, so I'll have most of August off."

"A pity you didn't have a bit of time off to help us with the hay." Martina thought her sister was their father's pet. She knew too that Darina liked farmwork as little as she did.

"Jobs are scarce enough. You can't walk out any time you like."

They were quiet for a while as Barbara negotiated the unfamiliar roads around Ennis. They were on the Galway road when Davoren asked. "Is TB contagious?"

"Such a question." Darina gave him an elbow in the ribs.

"A fair question," Johnny said. "The honest truth is I don't know." They all laughed when he put his hand in front of his mouth, as if to keep the germs away from them. "The doctors say it's not, and I'm sure they are right. It's not passed on easily anyway, but it obviously passes around among animals, seeing they are trying to get rid of it from cattle for thirty years now, without too much success."

"There are drugs now that were not there when TB was rampant years ago." Barbara gave a rundown on the sterling efforts made by Dr. Noel Browne, as Minister for Health, among others to improve people's conditions and fight tuberculosis at the end of the forties. The history lesson shortened the journey, and they were in Gort before they knew it. They stopped there for chips and burgers, and hardly noticed the other forty miles pass.

"It's great to be alive." Johnny stood at the front door, his hand on Davoren's shoulder, looking out at the sea. Barbara squeezed out beside her husband, hugged and kissed him.

"Stop that old stuff," Davoren said, "everyone will be looking."

"I hope they are," Barbara laughed. "I hope they are."

❦

Bishop Thomas Doherty went to Maynooth college for a few days. He wanted time to think, to clear his mind, discuss Pat Barrettt's situation with trusted colleagues. There was a lot of pressure coming on him from the media, looking for interviews, statements, his personal point of view. From the beginning he had put out the official version, that the church could not give in to blackmail, the long tradition of clerical celibacy in the Roman church, the parlous state of the church in the middle ages before compulsory celibacy was introduced, blah, blah, blah.

That worked for a while. It did not satisfy the journalists, but it kept them off his back. Day by day it now seemed that there was a danger of Barrett's strike having a knock on, domino type of effect. His action had struck a chord. Priests in various parts of the world were threatening hunger-strikes themselves if Pat was allowed to die. This information was privileged, but the papal nuncio, Dr. McIntosh had assured him the previous day that this was the type of feedback Rome was getting.

McIntosh was a big gruff Australian that Doherty could imagine as being more like a sheep farmer than a bishop. One of the wits among the hierarchy had christened him "Crocodile" and the name had stuck. Still he understood English, and you could talk to him, man to man, unlike some of his predecessors. The bishop remembered someone having referred to a previous nuncio and the collected bishops and their auxiliaries as "Alibrandi and the forty thieves."

"I wouldn't mind Tom," McIntosh had told him, "if these blokes making the threat were just ordinary bullshitters, you get those in any organisation. But these are the salt, Tom, as in 'of the earth.' This one could blow, unless you put a lid on it fast,"

"If I don't... I have done everything possible. This thing is driving me out of my mind. Help I came to look for."

"Look, Tom. We're talking damage limitation here. The boss cannot afford to be dragged into this thing. The damage has to be confined to a diocese, to a parish. The fire has to be quenched at base."

"I thought an Australian would be first to understand that there was not much point in quenching the spark that lit the fire, when the bush is already blazing."

"Point taken, Tom, but it's still in your hands. Use that legendary charm, and if the carrot doesn't work, try the stick."

"I'm seriously thinking of tendering my resignation."

"I can tell you right now, Tom that big papa will not accept. We anticipated, discussed that scenario before."

"Nobody can stop me resigning, getting out if I want to."

"You have it in one, mate, but what is it the Americans say? 'You won't eat in this town again.' There might be no room in the inn, ties might have to be cut completely. I gather you do want to remain in the priesthood. Don't get me wrong. I'm not saying that that is what would happen. Just that we need you, Tom, not just for this. We need men like you for the long haul."

"Life is all about carrots and sticks, isn't it? What stick do you see me using? The old crozier is a bit bent."

"Good one, Tom. Tell me, do you believe that man is sane?"

"Man for man, Pat Barrett is probably the best, the most idealistic priest I have."

"That is not the question I asked, Tom, and you know it."

"You think he should be committed to a psychiatric institution?"

"We still have some good Catholic doctors. The man needs attention, Tom."

"I think you should accept my resignation. I'm not prepared to stoop that low, even for the Pope's representative."

"Now, now, Tom, I didn't say you had to take that approach. You asked about carrots and sticks. I pointed out one."

"The ultimate in cynicism."

"We live in the real world, Tom. Even Peter and Paul got stuck in each other at one stage, according to Acts. Idealism is great, wonderful. We keep it out there on the horizon, something to aspire to. Down here," McIntosh tapped the table, "it's reality."

"Ever hear of the holy spirit?"

"Good one, Tom. Look. You and I are here to protect the ordinary Catholic, to preserve the organisation, because people need the organisation to protect, and help them hand on their faith."

"I didn't come into the "organisation" to defend the indefensible."

"It's a big mistake to try and make yourself bigger than the organisation"

"It's a bigger mistake to compromise your principles for the sake of the organisation."

"I don't think we are really in disagreement, Tom.

You and I don't make the rules. We put them into motion, into practice. We're not policy makers, just policy implementers."

They had not really got anywhere, only back to the the old cliché that he would "do his best" to find a solution. Thomas Doherty was depressed when he got down to Maynooth, but found that the atmosphere of the place lifted him as it always seemed to do. It was a home from home, where rooms are kept free at all times for bishops. He was glad the students were away. He needed space, time, thought. He could get food sent to his room so that he would not even have to meet staff.

Coming from a largely treeless part of the country, the tall trees of Maynooth had an inspiring quality for him ever since his student days. Their age impressed him too. One of them was even associated with Silken Thomas, centuries before the seminary was built. These had seen a few crises in their time. There was no crisis that did not pass.

He was sure of one thing. He was not putting Pat Barrett into any psychiatric institution. The resignation option was always there, but who would Pat have to deal with then? He liked this young radical priest, saw in him a courage he felt he did not have himself. Barrett had faith, strong faith, even if he did not always agree with church teaching. He knew that many of his parishioners called him a "críost eile" another Christ, precisely because he questioned as Jesus had questioned pharisee and scribe, because in all situations he seemed to ask what would Christ do in this case.

That was not to say that Barrett did not have his blind spots. His bishop had a good idea that he lived with a young woman. He did not know if that woman's child was his too, and he had asked no questions. The man was doing his job as well or better than the next. Everything would be alright except for that stupid celibacy rule. He knew that the fact that Teresa and her child had left Pat had a lot to do with his decision to go on strike. He was taking on a rule that had broken up his "marriage." Thomas Doherty understood his case well. He had been in love once too.

He could see Sally clearly now in his mind's eye, Sally as she was the year both of them were doing the "dip" in University College, Galway. The head of red hair, the teeth so white when she smiled, the flashing eyes. She was alive in a way he thought few people were alive. She glowed. Her language was often vulgar, almost always witty. She often shocked the ardent young cleric just out of Maynooth with some of the things she came out with. They became very friendly. He had been in love at a time a cleric was not supposed to even think of love except as a word in a sermon. He thought, both of them thought they could have a loving platonic relationship.

They had too, for a while. Because he lived in a college, and she with three other girls in a flat, they were able to be friends without ever physically touching each other, not two in one flesh but two of like mind. Then one Saturday he called to her flat. Although getting him a cup of tea, she seemed distant. "You know that it is all wrong." she said suddenly.

"I didn't realise you would be here on your own."

"That's not what I mean. It's a sin."

"I never laid a hand on you."

"It's a sin to be so great with a priest."

"You usen't be like this, Sally. What has got into

you?"

"I can't see you any more. It's a sin." Tears rolled slowly down her face.

"You have a boyfriend?"

"Isn't it little you know..."

He could no longer remember leaving the flat, how their breakup actually happened. He knew he had wanted to put his arms around her, but felt that would really be the sin. Fear of the physical had been driven into his marrow. In retrospect it was Sally that had made him a bishop. He was not going to be burned again. It was the straight and narrow from then on. He had thrown himself fully into his work in the college, eventually becoming president, the usual stepping stone to the episcopate in the diocese.

Years later Sally, a baldheaded husband and a clutch of redhaired children had joined him in a photograph after her youngest was confirmed. She had no grey rib, the same broad smile, that aura about her which was probably heightened by the crows feet below her sparkling eyes. For a mad moment he thought the young fellow he had confirmed had called him "daddy." He had been calling his father into the photograph. Wasn't she the lucky woman not to get me, he thought wryly.

A train rumbled by as he stood at the top of "graf" the straight walk to the south of the college. Thomas Doherty remembered the night during their pre-ordination retreat he and a couple of companions had thrown a tea chest full of Guinness bottles one by one across the wall into the canal that ran beside the railway. "I was not always the cute careful hoor I am often portrayed," he thought. "I might surprise the crocodile yet."

He felt better as he walked slowly back to his college room. A whiskey in his hand, he sat in the big armchair looking out on the well manicured square with the ivy-covered walls beginning to take on that reddish hue he always associated with autumn in Maynooth. "Damn McIntosh," he said aloud. "I know more about my priests, understand them better than I do the organisation, the institution. It was the institution of his day that crucified Jesus." Some kind of echo stirred in his mind—The institution was made for man, not man for the institution. As for woman...

❦

"It's easy guess what these two are up to." Neddy John Tom winked at his mates, Tomeen and Dara. The bearded man who had come in with the tall blonde girl had bought them a drink. "Newspaper reporters," he whispered.

"Sláinte." Dara raised his glass to the two young people who were warming themselves before the fire.

"Health, wealth and happiness," was Tomeen's wish for them. He let a "shush" out of him when he heard Neddy's loud whisper—"And may it not be long until ye do it again..."

"How are things up in the big smoke?" Neddy threw out a baited hook in an effort to find out who or what the visitors were.

"We stay as far away from the smoke as we can." The man's reply was of little help. The girl smiled at him, and reached up to wipe some Guinness froth from his moustache.

"That's a fine bit of growth you have there. It must be a great help to keep out the cold in winter."

Tomeen rubbed his chin to explain to the puzzled looking visitors what he was talking about.

"Summer and winter are all the same to me as far as that is concerned."

"You must have a fortune saved." Neddy stood aside as if to have a better look at the beard while he had an eyeful of the girl's bare miniskirted legs which were given extra prominence when she sat up on a high stool. "I'd safely say that it's a while since you bought a gilette?"

"It was not today or yesterday I let it grow, alright."

"I was walking out with an English girl myself during the war..." Neddy was just getting into full flow when Tomeen interrupted him.

"I thought it was beyond in France that you spent the war?"

"I wasn't in France all the time." Neddy gave him a withering look. "Have you never heard of french leave?"

"Never mind the war. Tell us about the woman." Dara tried to prevent another war. "A woman is more interesting than any war, especially when you have a confirmed bachelor talking about her. A bit like a fisherman talking about the one that got away."

"I never said any of them got away. I just was never interested enough to keep one of them as a souvenir."

"Tell us about your French friend." The girl spoke for the first time.

"It wasn't about the girl I was going to talk, but about her mother."

"You were going out with the mother as well?" Dara remembered an old rhyme "Brian O Linn and his wife, and wife's mother..."

"The woman in question..." Neddy put on his best

accent as he addressed the couple by the fire. "She had a beard on her as long as yours is any day."

"Are you sure it was a woman was in it?"

"What kind of an *amadán* do you take me for, Tomeen?"

"And had the daughter a beard?" Dara knew how to set up a good reply for his friend.

"She had no rib of hair on her anywhere. Her head was as bare as a child's arse."

"As bald as an egg?" After all the years Tomeen could still be taken in by one of Neddy's stories.

"Top and bottom." Neddy looked at his pint as if deep in reminiscence. The young couple giggled together, almost as if they were afraid to laugh out loud.

There was quiet in the bar for a few minutes, the local men sipping their pints, the visitors looking at the swirling flames among the turfsods. It was Tomeen who broke the silence, keeping his voice too low for the young couple to hear.

"Hasn't that one a great pair of goalposts? Bet you wouldn't mind scoring between them, Neddy." He rubbed his hands together. "Even this old cuckoo wouldn't mind laying an egg in that nest."

"I never went in for the blondes, the best day I was." Neddy slowly shook his head.

"That's not a real blonde." Tomeen said emphatically.

"He must have a better view than we have." Dara winked at Neddy. "Short and all as her skirt is... Legs up to her arse."

"Looking at the roots of her hair I was. And her eyebrows." Tomeen was serious. "Can't ye see that she is dark really?"

"Well, there is one way to find out, Tomeen."

"You're a married man, Dara."

"You hardly expect me to look. I'll just tell her you are curious, that you want to find out if she really is blonde."

"You wouldn't dare…Dara. Dara Nóra…" Tomeen thought he would die with embarrassment as Dara headed towards the fireplace, where he started to speak in a low voice to the strangers. Tomeen checked his run to the door, in case the bearded fellow came after him.

"Would you mind settling a bet for us?" Dara quietly asked the girl. "My friend over beyond claims that you read the news sometimes on the television, even though he cannot put a name on you. Would you mind telling us is he right?"

"I wish he was." She laughed, and waved over at Tomeen. "I'm afraid you've got it wrong. You'll have to look a bit closer the next time."

"Don't take a bit of heed of that fellow." Tomeen shouted over. "He never stops taking the mickey." He was embarrassed, but at least beardy had not lost his cool. Some fellows would accuse you of insulting their girlfriends for half as much.

"I wouldn't mind your wan taking my mickey all the same, blonde or not." Neddy seemed to be talking to himself, but he was talking too loud for Tomeen.

"Will you give over, for Jesus' sake, Neddy."

"What's wrong with you now?"

"If them are two journalists, they'll have it all over the papers that all we were interested was the colour of their hair, and the poor priest dying away up the road."

"I think we forget about them being journalists at

this stage."

"You're very sure of yourself, Neddy."

"It's not for nothing I was in the secret service. I'd lay a bet or two that those two young ones are on their honeymoon, or that they're down here for a dirty weekend."

"How do you make that out?"

"Can't you see the way they are looking at each other. Those two have only one thing in mind, and it's not chatting to Dara over there. Those two are cracked for a bit of *craiceann* as we used to call it in the old days." Neddy did not seem to be as sure of himself that the couple were not journalists when Dara came over to say the girl would like to take a picture of the three of them holding their pints "Are you out of your mind?" he asked.

"Surely you're not looking for money for your picture?" Dara asked.

"I don't want my picture in any paper."

"These are not for a paper." She held up her camera. "This thing only takes snapshots. They would not be good enough to publish in a newspaper."

"But they might be good enough to show to your boss."

"What has my boss to do with it?" she asked exasperatedly.

"How do I know that you're not some kind of guager?"

"Guager?" She looked at her friend who shook his head and shrugged his shoulders. Dara tried to explain. "We call the sort of person that checks up on a person's dole a guager around here. They are a very smart alecky crowd, and you wouldn't know how they would be trying to catch a person out. A lot of people have been cut back and some have left the country because of it." The bearded man began to laugh. He nudged his companion, "They think that we are some kind of secret service." She looked into his eyes and smiled.

"They are on their honeymoon alright." Neddy said.

"As a matter of fact we are. Monica here is an actress, and I happen to be a psychiatric nurse. We're the last people in the world that would be trying to stop your dole." The men were full of best wishes and half embarrassed apologies. Tomeen tried the old Irish blessing "*Sliocht sleachta ar shliocht bhur sleachta* " but made a hames of the aliteration.

"Speaking of the secret service, Jim," Monica said. "Tell them the one about Fidel Castro's secret service."

"It might not be the right kind of story for polite society."

"I wouldn't worry too much about that." She smiled at the men. "They seem to know all about pubic hair. I'm used to picking up prompts," she explained. Neddy looked a bit bewildered. "Would that have anything to do with the hair of the dog in the morning?" Nobody knew if he was serious or joking, but everyone laughed anyway.

"What about that story, Jim?" Dara asked.

"There was this Paddy over in Havana, and he went into a pub for a drop of rum. He paid for it and sat back to drink it. He noticed a lot of bearded soldiers drinking away but never seeming to have to pay for their drinks. The next time he was up at the bar he asked about it. "Fidel's army" the barman explained. Paddy took his drink, opened his fly, and said—"Fidel's secret service..."

"Wasn't there another good one about Fidel?" Tomeen asked. When neither of his companions could remember, he whispered something to Neddy. Comprehension dawned.

"You mean Fido?"

"It was as good a story as I ever heard."

"Let us have it," Monica said.

"I couldn't refuse anything to such a fine looking girl." Tomeen shook himself a bit, not being used to being the centre of attention. "There was this girl took home her intended to meet the family. He was a grand fellow, but he had a bit of a problem with the wind, farting like, very frequent. Things were going grand at the table until he couldn't hold on any longer and he let an awful rasper. The smell was awful, and sure nobody knew where to look. Your man was embarrassed to hell until he heard the man of the house saying 'Out Fido' to the dog. 'I'm alright,' said he to himself.'The dog will be blamed for everything.' The next time he let one the man of the house said the same thing—'Out Fido.' The dinner went on grand until they were at the dessert, and your man let another desperate rasper to the world.'Out Fido,' said the man of the house, 'before that fellow shits all over you.'"

Stories went back and forth between them away into the night. There was much laughter, none more so than when Tomeen asked—"Is this the best part of your honeymoon?"

There was serious talk too.

"You would feel guilty about laughing so much," Dara said at one stage, "and the priest dying at the other end of the village." When it emerged that Jim and Monica had heard nothing about Pat Barrett and his hunger-strike, it was Neddy who remarked wryly "You two are in love alright."

❧

Seamus, Mickey and Macdara were out training for the under twenty one *currach* races. They had won everything in the under eighteen category in the previous couple of years. Some of the older men were already mentioning them in the same breath as the great Joyces of Inis Bearachain, or the Folans or McDonaghs of Carraroe. Others claimed that this was like comparing Jack Dempsey with Mahomed Ali, an impossibility since they had never faced each other in competition. *Currach* racing was bigger in the west than hurling or football, but being a minority sport seldom merited mention in the city media.

"The shagger is hungover." Seamus remarked to Macdara. They felt that Mickey was not pulling his weight.

"I know the hangover he has." Macdara let his oars trail in the water. "Love. He's good for nothing since he started going with Aisling." He turned around to face Mickey. "That one has you rightly fucked."

"You can say that again," was Mickey's smug reply.

"Poor old Macdara is jealous," Seamus said. "No girlfriend of his own."

"Time enough."

"You would think you would ask Martina to go out with you."

"I'm no babysnatcher, Seamus."

"What does it matter if she has what it takes?" Mickey asked. "Isn't she the same age as Aisling? And nearly as sexy."

"Martina is a year younger even though they're in the same year up above." A nod of Macdara's head indicated the community school.

"That's one bird that's ripe for the plucking if there ever was one, but she has a tongue in her as sharp as a nail." Mickey lit himself a cigarette as the *currach* drifted slowly in an almost calm sea. "She nearly took the head off me at the dance the last night."

"She has an awful hatred of the drink." Seamus said. "She gives out hell to Darina about me having a few now and again. There's no stopping her at all now that I tipped the car the last night."

"They're all against everything until they get the taste." Mickey dragged on his cigarette. "Then there's no stopping them."

"Whatever about the women, Mickey," Seamus said. "Fags are no help to your rowing."

Mickey ignored him, continuing to ask Macdara about Martina. "I have no doubt at all but that she fancies you," he said. "She couldn't keep her eyes off you the other night."

"Sure she's going out with Colm."

"Puppy love," said Mickey contemptuously. "If she's so hot on him, where was he the night they had the dance for her father?"

"How would I know? I think that it's yourself that fancies her the way you are going on about her."

"Leave me out of it. I'm well enough looked after, but Martina is there for the taking, good looks, and plenty of money now as well."

"I wouldn't say that too loud," Seamus said. "They are very sensitive about that collection."

"Sensitive? A pity someone wouldn't collect some for me. I wouldn't be too sensitive about it."

"You know how it is all the same. If it was your own father..."

"My father," Mickey said, "wouldn't give a fuck so long as he had the price of a few pints."

"Finish that coffin nail," Seamus said to him, "We're supposed to be practising."

"What's this TB anyway?" Mickey ignored him.

"TB or not TB, that is the question," Macdara said. "Who says that I didn't learn my Shakespeare?"

"One line anyway." Seamus was getting impatient. "To row or not to row is the question here and now." Mickey suddenly threw away the butt of his cigarette, and grabbed his oars. "What are ye waiting for?"

❦

The blessed virgin was shaking her head at Pat Barrett, telling him that he had got it all wrong, that it was not she who had told him to go on hunger-strike. She smiled at him then, told him not to worry. She would give him bread from her basket, wine from the jug that balanced on her head. "Man does not live on bread alone," she joked. "Neither does woman. We enjoy the drop of wine too."

He was sure she would spill the wine, the way she lowered her head. There seemed to be no cork, no cap on the jug. He reached out to catch it. He awoke. He felt convinced that he should give up the hunger-strike. The ironic thing was that nobody had allowed for a quick decision to quit. There was no food in the house, and he was too weak to walk to his neighbours. He wondered was the dream some kind of tease, a "turn these stones into bread" temptation, or was it just an indication of gut hunger. In a way, though he felt it a much clearer message than the original insight he had at the grotto, the insight that had sparked his fast.

He cast his mind back again to that May evening as he listened to the rosary, distraught at Teresa's decision to leave. He had prayed as he never prayed before, asked for a sign, something to show what God wanted for him, what Mary would have wanted from her son for him... It had come to him as a blinding flash of inspiration. Make celibacy a life or death issue in the church. Storm the Bastille. Take them on from the highest to the lowest. Make something of his life, his death.

If Mary said something like this at Fatima, Lourdes, even Knock, would not the Catholics of the world sit up and listen, even if the church did not insist on belief in marian apparitions? But of course she had said nothing. He had just thought it. But was that not in itself some kind of vision, some kind of inspiration? Or was he just losing his mind?

Again he thought that even if there was no element of inspiration involved, did not the logic of the situation demand that something drastic be done. More than a hundred thousand had left the ordained ministry, mostly because of this issue. Was it not time to pressurise the church authorities to face up to this stupid rule that deprived a quarter of the church of eucharistic ministry.

In a matter of minutes Pat Barrett was as convinced of his cause as he had been a few moments previously that he should come off his hunger-strike. His mind, or was it his emotions were like a pendulum swinging from side to side. The image in his mind was of the great iron ball on a crane used to knock tall buildings, a destructive pendulum swinging between heart and head and in danger of destroying both.

Why should a dry theory be more important to him than the love of woman? Love of Teresa and Jennie. How could a man crucified two thousand years ago have such a grip on a person that he could be allowed come between a man and a woman who wanted to live in love? Was he just living in a dream world?

But Teresa was real. A man should stick to what was real, and to hell with the theories, the spirits, the self-appointed gods. If the spirit could only be grasped, be wrestled...He looked at his hands. They could not catch the spirit, but somehow he felt that the spirit was in them. They were hands made more for a shovel than for a chalice, but they could bring Christ to being on an altar. Or could they? Was it God who was really the slippery serpent...?

Teresa and Jennie. Real people. They stood out clearly now before the eyes of his mind. Instead of brushing them aside in order to avoid the pain as he had done for so long, he allowed himself look lovingly at them. They were before him as they were that day Teresa brought home her baby, mother and daughter still as one although the umbilical chord had been cut. He loved them.

Why had Teresa been different from the other girls who had stayed with him during pregnancy? Madeleine and Joan were still friends although he saw little enough of them since Joan married and Madeleine had moved to the city. Maybe the difference was that they had remained in touch with the fathers of their children. Joan had always intended to marry Jimmy, but her parents would not sign the consent form until she was eighteen. Madeleine was older, very independently minded, opposed in principle to marriage, although he had got a hint in her last phonecall that she was now considering it for legal and security reasons, in a registry office of course. He had joked that he would be available anytime, when she came around to his way of thinking. "Anytime" did not seem so long anymore.

Teresa had no contact with Jennie's father, and Pat had slipped unconsciously into that role, a role he thoroughly enjoyed. He remembered with amusement his first blundering attempts at nappy-changing, though he had soon learned. Had to learn, he used to tease Teresa, or the poor child would be smothered in shit. "It's the least you might do, FATHER," she used to say.

Of course people had advised him that he was living dangerously when girls had first come to stay during pregnancy. He, she, or both of them would fall in love. Playing with fire, all that stuff. He didn't believe it, didn't care, thought himself too strong, was naive enough to think that God would somehow prevent it to protect his priest. Maybe it had all been the will of God.

Ironically enough it was in Maynooth college, one of the major training seminaries in the world for the priesthood, though now a university open to all, that he had got to know women, or felt he had. There were now more women than men in the college and they got on very well generally with the student priests. Pat Barrett felt that this gave him the experience to have women friends without becoming involved on a sexually physical level. But then there was a big difference between sharing a college with thousands of others and living on your own in a remote country parish.

Because Teresa was no longer involved with Jennie's natural father, because she did not know at the time if she could face her mother and family, because he was probably already in love with her, it seemed natural that they should stay with him after the birth of the baby. It would help him understand parenting better he had said. It was just until she would get on her feet. Any reason, every reason except the real one. They were in love.

He wondered now how they had managed to live under the same roof for so long without even touching physically. It was as they checked Jennie one night at bedtime that Teresa had accidentally brushed against him. He had caught her shoulders, held her to him, kissed her. "Where did you learn to do that?" she had asked laughingly.

"I read all the books."

"It wasn't in any book you learned to do that." They kissed, and kissed, and kissed. It was too late to turn back, and who wanted to turn back anyway?

He could not remember now at what stage that Teresa had become restless, that she had begun to talk of security a lot, of recognition. He knew too that she felt guilty, that love is no match for old-fashioned Catholic guilt.

Pat Barrett tried to rinse his mouth with water without letting the edges of the glass touch his lips. He ended up spilling some of it down his chest. While trying to wipe it dry he realised that his ribs were beginning to stand out like a skeleton. The decision for life or for death was increasingly imminent. Instinctively he knew that he would have to choose life, if only because of his fear of death. Had the Long Kesh hunger-strikers been as confused as he was, he wondered. He would have to give up. But he would hold out a while longer, try to rescue some dignity from the shambles while wriggling off the hook he had hung himself up on.

❧

Darina and Martina McKay travelled to Croagh Patrick in the front seat of Seamus' old Cortina, with Mickey, Aisling and Macdara in the back. Davoren would have liked to have gone too, but there was not enough room. His father promised to bring him the following year when he would be strong enough. As a consolation he offered to stand in goal while Davoren practised his hurling, but Barbara would have none of it. "When the doctor says you can, I'll give you my blessing as well," was her last word on the subject.

Darina was less than comfortable sitting on a cushion over the handbrake for the long journey, but she did not mind as she was beside Seamus. Macdara joked that he changed gears a lot more than necessary for the sake of "having a feel."

"If I want a feel, I don't need any excuse, but these roads are so crooked that you cannot travel very far without changing down."

"I believe you," Macdara joked, "but thousands wouldn't." They were all in high good humour, the coming climb as much an adventure as a pilgrimage.

"I'm not having half the feel those other two in the back are having." Seamus said.

"We're not doing anything." Aisling extricated herself from Mickey's arms and straightened herself up so that she could look out at the strange mountainy countryside.

"I have ye covered, in my mirror."

"Keep your eyes on the road or we'll all be in shit creek." Aisling looked down on Killary harbour, as the car snaked along the road built into the mountainside above it.

"If Croagh Patrick is as high as those ones, I don't know if we'll be fit for it at all." The climb was beginning to worry Macdara. "The women anyway..."

"The women anyway..." Darina half turned in her seat. "The women might show you a clean pair of heels."

"At least we have a bit of training done. For the races."

"Drink and fags training." Martina said it with less than her usual sarcasm on the subject. She enjoyed being out with the gang, although she had worried a lot before coming with them. She felt somehow grown-up.

"Don't worry girls," Mickey said. "We'll carry you on our backs if we have to."

"Let's ask the expert." Darina put her arm across Seamus' back. "You are the only one of us that has climbed it already."

"I like it," he said, indicating her arm, "but one driver might be enough on a road like this. The worst part of the mountain is the last half mile or so. The rest isn't much different than walking across a bog. I was only thirteen or fourteen at the time. Along with my father."

"So long as it was not with a girl, I don't mind."

"Sure life was nothing until I met you."

"Maybe the rest of us should get out and walk,"

Macdara said. "I think we are only in the way. This thing is getting awful intimate."

"What is it but a biteen of a hill?" was Mickey's comment when he got his first view of Patrick's holy mountain as the rounded a turn somewhere around Carrowkennedy.

"By the time you are on top," Darina said, "it may be high enough for you."

They were in a queue of cars, bumper to bumper when they turned west just before reaching Westport. "Look at all the islands." Macdara cleared some condensation from the back window on the right.

"Three hundred and sixty-five. One for every day of the year." Seamus said.

"And an extra one every leap year," Martina quipped.

"Really?" Mickey was fascinated.

"Pull my other leg, Martina," Aisling had a scathing ring to her voice. Macdara tried to come to Martina's help by making a case for a leap year's spring tide revealing more submerged islands than the usual. It did not sound very convincing, but Martina smiled her thanks to him.

They stretched themselves in the car park, glad of the space after being cooped up inside the car for nearly three hours, the last hour spent crawling along at snail's pace because of the volume of traffic. "I didn't think there were as many cars in the world," Martina said.

"This is just one of the car parks. When you think that there are forty or fifty thousand people climbing today. " Macdara stood beside her, as they looked up at the blue pyramid of a mountain Saint Patrick was reputed to have fasted on fifteen hundred years previously, but a holy mountain for long before that, so much so that the pilgrimage Sunday is still called after the old pagan god—"Domhnach Chrom Dubh." In the West of Ireland it is known mainly as Reek Sunday.

They joined the flow of people on the narrow pathway. The noise and movement would seem to suggest a cattle market more than a pilgrimage, souvenir medals and leaflets on sale along the way as well as minerals, sandwiches and chocolate, not to mention the ashplants to help with the climb. "Sticks for the Reek, sticks for the Reek, you can't attempt the Reek without a stick." The sellers reminded Darina of the newspaper men in Dublin "Press or 'Erald, Herald or Press." She felt they could be the same people, on their day off.

"Stick yere sticks." Mickey said contemptuously as he passed. The others, on Seamus' advice, since he had climbed before, bought a stick each.

"Remember it's not a race we're in." Seamus seemed to naturally assume command. "No heroics. Look out for each other. It is easy to fall or break an ankle. Take it easy."

"OK, captain." Mickey saluted sarcastically. He took Aisling's hand. When she saw Seamus put his arm around Darina, Martina slipped on ahead, in case she would be expected to hold Macdara's hand. It was not that she did not like him, but she thought she would feel embarrassed. Anyway it was not for the crack she had come on the pilgrimage, but to pray for her father's health. She was going to pray for Father Pat too, their school chaplain, whom she liked very much. Nobody wanted to see him die, and God would have to find a way out for him.

Martina reached the statue of Saint Patrick before the others and stood looking up at the greyblue mountain. Curls of mist floated about it here and there, as if some great giant lay smoking his pipe in the valley below. There was a magic about it all. Her eyes traced the pathway ahead, which at that stage seemed to wind away from the actual mountain. It was black with people, a continual human stream of all ages, shapes and sizes, the farthest of them looking no bigger than flies. She knew that the climb would be tough. She knew too that she was strong, hardened by the summer farmwork, fitter than Darina or Aisling, having been out in the air while one of them sat in an office and the other washed dishes in a hotel kitchen.

"Are you tired already?" Macdara stood beside her.

"Just waiting for the rest of you. Seamus said to stick together."

"Let's go. They are not far behind us. We'll wait for them after a while. Every step we climb is one less to go." She followed him, weaving from side to side on the rough rocky path, following the figures immediately in front, not saying much. A strong stream of water rushed down the hill just to the right of the path. The image of people going against the current occurred to Martina. That was what they were at, climbing a mountain when they could be tucked up comfortably in their beds. But there was a great comraderie among the crowd, some quietly praying, rosary beads slipping through young or gnarled fingers. Others shouted jubilantly. "Ooh, la la's" echoed up from the valley. Young people, old people, barefoot people, some wellingtoned, coated, others in t-shirts and jeans, many young men shirtless, men, women, children. It was great to be alive and among them, despite the sweat and the stress on calf and thigh as they climbed relentlessly.

They stopped on a little plateau after what they guaged to be half a mile, and sat on stones just off the pathway to wait for the others. When they had time to look around it was strange to see sheep eating contentedly among the heather so close to the human stream. But they would be used to people. It was not just on the official pilgrimage "Garland Sunday" that people climbed "the Reek." There was a constant stream of pilgrims, or just mountain climbers all summer long.

When the others caught up with them it was clear that it was Aisling that found the climb hardest. Her face looked yellow, and she had already been sick.

"Wasn't I the idiot to have eaten a breakfast, but my mother insisted."

"Have a cigarette, and get the taste out of your mouth." Mickey's idea of a cure sounded worse than the sickness, and even Aisling laughed.

"I'll be alright when I have a bit of a rest." she said. Darina was doubtful. Aisling's colour worried her. "Maybe you should just go back, and wait at the car. I'll go with you."

"You won't get out of it that easily." Seamus had said it when he realised it was too serious a matter to be flippant about.

"Let the rest of ye go on," Mickey suggested. "We'll rest awhile, and follow after a bit. Wait for us there at the highest point you can see from here. If we don't catch up with you after a quarter of an hour, go ahead without us." They all agreed on that, the other four facing the long hill, meeting an increasing flow of pilgrims on their way down, in high good spirits because the worst was over as far as they were concerned.

"You're almost there," some of them shouted, although their eyes told them otherwise. Others tried to depress them by saying they had hardly started yet. They knew that the truth lay somewhere in between. They waited at the point indicated by Mickey, but moved on when he and Aisling did not arrive. Legs were suddenly given a welcome relief when they reached a little valley where the ground was pleasantly boggy. Seamus pointed out a little lake which seemed to perch incongruously on the side of the mountain.

"That is *tóin ifrinn*, he said, hell's hole, or should I say hell's arse? That's where Saint Patrick is supposed to have put the snakes." He fired a stone which spread ripples in the little lake, no more than a big pond. "You are supposed to throw a stone into that on the way down, my father said the last time we were here."

"We are only on the way up yet," Darina reminded him. "Anyway it's all superstition, *pisreog*..."

"It's a nice *pisreog* all the same." Seamus threw another stone. "You should give hell to the devil every chance you get."

"It might be better not to disturb him at all," Macdara commented.

"Are we going to stay here all day?" Martina was worried that they might be away too long from Aisling, if help was needed.

"It's like trying to climb a wall," Darina said when they came to the most difficult part of the mountain. "Only worse. There would be no stones sliding down a wall." It reminded Macdara of the *duirling*, the rocky stormbeach by the sea, if it were set up at a seventy five degree angle.

"Another hundred yards," someone on their way down said.

"Start counting." Macdara had a plan. "Count to a hundred. Even if each step is only a foot because it's so steep, we'll make it in three goes of a hundred."

"But you are not allowing for the slippage. Three steps here is only as good as one normally." Seamus was not convinced of the value of counting.

"It will take our minds off the climbing." Martina supported Macdara. "Come on. One two three." She set out in a scramble, but found herself slipping back against Macdara a moment later. He gave her an almost imperceptible hug of encouragement.

"Thanks," she smiled, and he winked at her. Her step seemed lighter. Her heart certainly was as he stayed by her side, giving her a support to hang on to any time she felt herself slipping. Macdara was completely on all fours now, concentrating on counting his steps, Martina doing the same. They stopped after the first hundred to wait for Darina and Seamus. "The two of you are like frogs," Darina said, as they lay, breathless and laughing on the side of the mountain.

The downward rush of people seemed to intensify as they lay watching. When Macdara suggested moving ahead another hundred, Seamus told him to give it a few more minutes.

"A Mass has probably just finished up above. When the crowd thins out we will have a go at it, all four together, all for one and one for all." It was like one of his morale boosting speeches before a *currach* race. He was right though. The pilgrims' way cleared considerably, and they set out again, counting, one hundred, two, three. When they stopped the third time Martina looked up and saw the white gable of the little church. She gave a yell of delight.

They reached the top a few minutes later, and threw themselves on the ground until the pains left their muscles and bones. A Mass was just beginning in the open air at the gable wall of the church. A huge crowd of people stood or sat around about, while others circled the chapel, doing "stations." Martina stood up when she had rested.

"It's not half high enough," she joked.

"Sssssh. Pay heed to the Mass." Darina spoke in a cross whisper.

"Whatever you say mammy." Martina was pleased to see that Macdara enjoyed her joke. She had no doubt at the same time that it was the most enjoyable Mass she was ever at. There had been so much effort involved in getting there, an element of challenge, of sacrifice involved, not like wandering down to the local church on a Saturday night or Sunday morning.

At the same time Darina was thinking that she saw a side of Seamus she had seldom seen before, strong, caring, reflective.

"I like this Seamus," she whispered.

"What Seamus?"

"Seamus, the holy Joe." She laughed out loud.

"Have a good look. It might be a long time before you see him again."

"Has anybody a notion of going home?" Macdara stood up and blessed himself. The Mass was over.

"Wait a minute until we see the view." Darina led the way to the edge of the mountain. It seemed strange that the top which in the distance looked like a triangle point in the sky was in fact as big as a football field. They looked down on the great expanse of Clew

Bay, guarded at the entrance by the great shoulders of Grainuaile's Clare Island. Other islands dotted the bay, with Achill stretching out into the Atlantic across from them. To the southwest, a rosary of islands, some inhabited, some not, Turk and Boffin among them, stretched down by the coast. North and south of them was pockmarked with mountains, while to the east stood the plains of Mayo, boggy or forested plains it seemed from that vantage point. They set out for the descent when they had feasted their eyes on what must be one of the finest views in the country, a view too often shrouded in mist.

They slipped. They slid. They fell on their bums again and again. They went down slowly, two by two, making sure that when they fell, they fell on their backs. "Keep your weight as near the ground as you can," Seamus was saying again and again. After a while they developed a pattern, a few sliding steps, stop, slide ahead again and stop. It seemed as if it would never end, the only consolation being that at least they were on the way down. Martina felt a kind of pity for those still on the way up. The worst was before them still.

At last they reached the little glen beneath "the hard part," as everyone called it. Sitting on the heathery bank beside the pathway they ate oranges, laughed and joked, each one proud of his or her personal achievement, even if they were just one of fifty thousand climbers on the day.

"Macdara must have you murdered," Seamus said to Martina. "He was in a heap on top of you everytime I looked at the two of you."

"I'd have been killed without him," was her reply.

"All he was looking for was an excuse to jump on

top of you."

"Shut your big mouth." Macdara spoke with a mixture of anger and embarrassment.

"He didn't fall on me half often enough." Martina caught and gently squeezed his hand.

"What have we here?" Darina raised her voice. "The beginning of a beautiful romance?"

"Fuck off," her sister said with a smile. "Come on." She caught Macdara's arm. "We have to throw a couple of stones into *tóin ifrinn*."

They went down nearly as far as the statue in about half an hour's brisk walk. it was then they caught up with Mickey as he walked slowly behind a stretcher carried by Order of Malta men. Aisling lay on the stretcher, obviously in severe pain, her face extremely pale.

"What is wrong with her?" Darina asked one of the uniformed men.

"We're not certain, but she does seem to be having a miscarriage. She has lost some blood. There is a doctor on the way, and a helicopter to take her to Castlebar hospital."

"A miscarriage?" Darina half exploded in laughter. "That's impossible. She is only sixteen."

"I shouldn't have mentioned it at all." The man seemed annoyed with himself. "I thought her friends would know." Darina looked at Martina, who shrugged in an "I don't know" way. Mickey said that the ambulance men, as he called them didn't know their arses from their elbows. "Wait until the real doctor comes. It's just some kind of a haemorrhage."

When Martina tried to take Aisling's hand to try and console her, she was rebuffed by a quick push off. "Suit yourself." Martina said haughtily.

"What will you tell her mother?" Darina asked Martina in a loud whisper.

"Why should I have to tell her?"

"You're her friend."

"Mickey is her friend."

"It's probably only an appendix." Mickey repeated aloud to no one in particular.

In a matter of minutes after reaching the level ground Aisling was whisked away in a helicopter from one of the carparks. "What do we do now?" Darina asked.

"What can we do except go home?" Seamus was opening the car door. He asked Mickey—"Do you want us to follow her to the hospital?"

"It has nothing to do with me." He sat into the car. The others looked at each other across the roof, shrugged, sat in. There was hardly a word from anyone on the long, anticlimactic journey home.

❦

"Five and five and five" Cóilín a' Phortaigh could not count past five, but that in itself was enough for him. Enough to know that all his sheep were there. He had never had an opportunity to go to school apart from a few days before communion and confirmation. His father had been old when he married. He had died when Cóilín was seven. As the only child he had been needed at home to help his mother on land and shore. The parish priest had come twice and a guard once to try and make him go to school. They had threatened prison but nothing ever came out of it except that he had feared priests and guards. That was until Neddy John Tom had told him that there was a nice priest in the village now, that he would advise him well. That was the time the dole was taken off him, and they had given him de Valera's pension.

Neddy was the one he met most when he was out on the *muirbheach*, the flat sandy part between the sea and the bog. The grass was scarce there but there were good pickings in it for his few sheep. Although this was commonage to which many farmers had a claim, very few used it apart from Cóilín and Neddy, whose cow could be found in the same place every day at its master's milking time. Once a day Neddy did his milking, and strangely enough any cow he ever had became accustomed to the habit. He milked about midday, to leave the evening free for the love of his life, the pub.

That was the time Cóilín would go to see him if he wanted information about something, to have a letter collected from the post office, or sometimes his pension and a few groceries. It was to enquire about his friend, the priest that Cóilín approached Neddy.

"Sure how would I know, Cóilín? You saw him since I did. I haven't seen him since he stopped saying the Mass."

"But there would be talk of him in the public house?"

"When did the truth ever come from a public house?" Neddy ground tobacco with the heel of one hand in the palm of the other.

"He hasn't started eating yet?"

"Not that I have heard of."

"The hunger is a quare thing."

"Sure we all had to put up with it long ago. Now that the food is in it, they're not eating it, between the slimmers and the hunger-strikers."

"Still I wouldn't like there to be anything on Father Pat."

"I wouldn't either, Cóilín, but there's little you or me can do about it. It's himself has chosen it, himself that's doing it."

"They say that it's all on account of a woman."

"You or me got no woman, Cóilín, and we didn't go on any hunger-strike."

"Sure maybe it's a pity we didn't."

Neddy drew a cross with the froth of the milk on the cow's side when he had finished milking. "Why don't you come down to the village with me, Cóilín, and have a few drinks? You can call in on your mate, Father Pat, on the way." Cóilín was a bit fidgety.

"I'm not so sure they would let me in. I was never there that the priest was not with me. Beartla's father threw me out long ago..."

"That was then. This is now. If they don't let you in, I'll never darken the door of that place again. Or my mates either."

"I have a bit of a dryness on me alright."

"Let's hit the road so."

ৼ

Teresa Carter decided that it was time to set out for the city. She wanted to have a flat booked well before the September glut of students would start house and flat hunting. There were a few points to be cleared up too with the university, about grants and other entitlements. Although she was only going away overnight she felt that she was in some way breaking a link with Jennie. It was not that her mother wouldn't look after her as well or better than herself when she went to college. It was the beginning of a journey in a new direction, full of fears and worries.

Teresa had no doubt at the same time but that she was doing the right thing. It was just that she did not know would she be fit for it. Would she have forgotten all she had learned in secondary school? Would she be able to study after four years in which she had read nothing but novels and newspapers? If she were to fail after all her efforts, Jennie fully depending on her? Then, all of a sudden the lump of sadness that had been in her throat as she walked down the road disappeared when the bus came.

"So what, if I fail itself," she said to herself. "My mother managed to rear a big family without benefit of university. I have my health. There are plenty of jobs I can do. I'm not afraid of work, of cooking, cleaning...I can earn my keep on my back if I have to." She started to laugh out loud at that thought. The man in the seat opposite looked at her as if she had a screw loose. With a bravado that surprised her she winked at him. He raised his newspaper, but seemed unable to read it as the bus shook and shuddered on the potholed roads. He spent the rest of the journey looking out the window, anywhere except at Teresa.

The idea of being away overnight, away without Jennie for the first time in the child's life, virtually, began to seem attractive. As much as Teresa loved her it was somewhat of a relief not to have her hanging out of her skirts the whole time. Not that she had been much of a mother lately, but the day at the beach seemed to have changed all that. It was as if she was beginning to live again. It was almost as if she had forgotten how young she was. It would be nice to be able to go to a film or a nightclub again. She could not spend all her time studying. The week would be broken up nicely, four nights in the city, the weekend at home with her mother and Jennie.

Although she told herself continuously that she would stay away from men forever, she never doubted for a moment that she could meet with, love someone again. Would anyone stand comparison with Pat? But that would change too. Time changed everything. She remembered the time her father died, the other big grief in her life. She had thought that she would never laugh again, never enjoy anything. But that changed too. Time. She rarely thought of him now except at anniversaries. It was not as if she no longer loved him, just that she no longer needed to grieve. The same would happen with Pat. Or would it?

He was still there, so close. The first thing she had thought when she winked at your man across the way was—"I'll have to tell this to Pat." For a second time that morning a lump of sadness, formed in her throat. "Didn't I give him a hard time too," she thought, "jealousy, jealousy without any reason most of the time, especially when Madeleine came around. It was different with Joan, the other girl that had stayed with Pat during pregnancy, because Jimmy used come with her. But Madeleine was independent, vivacious, full of ideas of how to organise your life for you. Worst of all of course was when the bitch called Pat "love" or "pet."

The ironic thing was that their children got on great. "We'll have a wedding here yet," Madeleine used to say. "The romance has started already." "Not if I can help it," Teresa had heard herself mutter. Imagine getting worked up about kids of two or three years of age... But of course Pat could see no reason at all for her jealousy. "There is so much love between the two of us," he used to say, "that nothing on earth can come between us." He was right. It was not this life, but the next that had come between them, "that and holy mother church."

Although Teresa raged and railed about the church's law of celibacy she had come to the conclusion that there was a lot of sense to it, that is if it were not allowed to break people's hearts. Again and again she had felt that Pat Barrett's commitment to herself and Jennie had come between him and the commitment he might have given the poor or the missions. Although he reassured her that this was not so, she had felt that they were somehow holding him back from his real vocation. That too was part of the reason she had left him. Only for him to turn around and start a stupid hunger-strike. She loved him, but, O Jesus, she was so mad with him. But her new life was starting now, today...

Teresa managed to sort out her business in the university in less than half an hour. The girl in the office was as efficient as she was polite. She hoped that finding accommodation would be as easy. She had to tell herself again to calm down, not to be nervous, that she was only four years out of circulation. Everything new was not necessarily a problem. She decided to have a cup of coffee in an old mill restored as a shopping complex, to sit by the river, watch the swans, relax while looking through the advertisements in the local papers. She drew a ring around the more attractive looking possibilities. She wanted a place within walking distance of the college. The money she would save on bus fares might mean a more congenial lodgings.

Half an hour on the phone reduced her shortlist to three. Most of the others had already been booked in the couple of days since the papers had been published. As it happened the first place she looked at turned out to be the most suitable, but she was not to find that out until she had the feet walked off herself. Teresa felt that her mother's hens were better housed than in one foul smelling excuse for a flat she was offered. The other was luxurious but too expensive. The first one, and the one she eventually chose had a small neat room with a kitchen cum sitting room to be shared with two others. They were out at the moment, the landlady said, one working, the other up in the college library studying for the repeats.

They would both be in around six, she said, and advised Teresa not to pay a deposit until she had met them.

"I don't mind who they are or what they are like at this stage. This is the best I have seen. Unless they have contagious diseases or something, I will put up with them. It's not for the socialising or the crack that I'm here, but for the study."

"That's what they all say," the landlady laughed, "though the students seem to be improving by the year, concentrating on the study a lot more like. There was a time they would burn the staircase on you as firewood, but I don't suppose that you're like that."

"Is that why you have no open fire?" For a moment Teresa felt that she had insulted the woman, but she just laughed her hearty laugh. "Don't worry about the heat, dear. There's a fine central heating system. The meter for the oil is over here."

It came as something of a shock to Teresa when the first of her flatmates came in, a young man with a ponytail and a little triangle of a beard on his chin. He had a bundle of law books under his arm. "Shake with Jake." He offered his hand.

"I thought I was sharing with girls. She never said..."

"What have we got here? A manhater?"

"It's just that it never occurred to me."

"Each has a room of his or her own," he said grandly, "and anyway Jake is outnumbered, blessed among women. Sinéad will be home shortly. Tea or coffee?"

Sinéad seemed to be as zany as Jake when she came in with a theatrical flourish, fell on her knees with her arms across her chest, and said "Am I about to die, now that this woman has come to take my Jake away from me?" Teresa began to regret having paid her deposit, but before the end of the evening was enjoying their game, even felt as if she had always known them. She was going to enjoy university.

☙

Some days after returning from Croagh Patrick Barbara McKay agreed to bring Darina and Martina to Castlebar hospital to visit Aisling. Seamus seemed to have too many other things to do. Mickey said it had nothing to do with him. Aisling's parents were non-communicative. When the girls threatened to hitch there themselves, Barbara thought it better to bring them. There were too many stories of girls who hitched lifts being molested.

The car had scarcely disappeared around the first bend before Johnny and Davoren were heading for the haggard behind the hayshed, hurleys in hand. It was a good place to practise, empty until the harvest would be gathered in, the broad back of the shed preventing the ball from sailing away too far, two of the girders acting as goalposts. Johnny felt it would be no pressure on him to act as goalkeeper. All he had to do was stand there and try to stop the ball.

"I'll have to widen the goalposts for you," was Johnny's comment when Davoren's first effort sailed about a yard wide. His next shot was struck with such force and accuracy that his father did not even see it before it crashed off the wall behind him. "Not bad for a fluke," Johnny joked.

"Maybe this is a fluke too." Davoren's pride was so stung that he blasted another shot to the bottom right hand corner of what would be the net in a game situation. "Too flukes out of three ain't bad."

"God between us and the American accent..." Davoren tried to lob his father with a looping shot, but it was saved easily. When Johnny saved two of the next three efforts with deft flicks of his hurley, he asked proudly "What do you think of that for an old fellow? The eye is not gone yet." Lest his father should think that he was losing his touch Davoren shot three goals with his next three shots. When Johnny leapt to his left to save the next one at the foot of the girder he drew a "Not bad." from his son. He dropped his hurley and applauded his father, half seriously, half jokingly. Johnny got up gingerly, feeling weak, but he did not say anything.

He collapsed during a half-hearted effort to save the next shot.

"Come here until I lift you." Davoren thought for a moment that his father was playacting. Then he was struck by a mixture of guilt and worry. He rushed over and was even more shocked when he saw a trickle of blood from the corner of Johnny's mouth, a deep red against the pale face. "Oh, God, I'm sorry..."

"Don't worry, Dav. I'll be alright," Johnny said weakly. "Send for the doctor, good man. I'll be OK here." In the rush to the nearest house with a phone, Davoren was lucky not to fall off his bike twice, fearing the worst, wondering should he call the priest, "but what good would he be, and him dying himself?" he thought. The doctor would know best. An even bigger shock awaited him when he got back to the haggard to find that his father was no longer there. It all seemed like a bad dream. Then the thought came to him that he could not have moved unless he was able to walk. That was reassurance, a feeling which evaporated when he saw how weak his father looked as he lay on the couch in the living room.

"Would you like a cup of tea?" Davoren was almost afraid to raise his voice in case it would cause more damage.

"Just a drink of water. Good man." Johnny tried to smile, to reassure him but it came over as a weak grin. As Davoren was getting the drink the doctor's car ground to a halt in a crunch of gravel outside. After examining Johnny he rang for an ambulance on his handphone. When he saw the tears welling in Davoren's eyes, he told him that his father was in no danger, but that he would need to be hospitalised for a while. A young, kind man, the doctor showed him how to use the handphone, telling him he could ring anyone he liked.

"I don't want to ring anyone, really."

"What about Patricia?" Johnny asked laughingly.

"Patricia?" The doctor said. "Is that the girlfriend?"

Davoren cringed with embarrassment.

"She's a bit long in the leg for him," his father said, "but I'm sure your crowd would have no bother cutting a few inches of bone from her shins."

"Don't mind him," The doctor put his hand on Davoren's shoulder. "He's not too bad when he's able to take the piss. And don't worry about the size. You'll shoot up past that girl and everyone else in a few years. Girls of your age are always taller than boys. Ye start to grow up and they start to grow out." He shaped his hands like breasts on his chest. Davoren didn't know what to think. He was used to stuff like that from boys of his own age, but not from grownups. Still he liked the perkiness and kindness of the man. Maybe he would be a doctor himself.

Davoren played down the hurling as much as possible when his mother and sisters came back a few hours after Johnny had been removed to the university college hospital.

"Put on something clean," Barbara told him, "and we'll go straight in to see him. At least we might be let into this hospital. The other journey was in vain, strict orders from Aisling's parents to let no one but family see her."

❧

Pat Barrett thought that Eugene Johnson was the nicest media person to interview him so far. He had known the man's work for quite some time, as he freelanced for various publications. He had the reputation of knocking the mighty from their seats and exalting the lowly, to quote the magnificat. Pat held him in a kind of awe, and though warned to be careful with him, felt it an honour that such a journalist should be interested enough to come all the way from Dublin to interview him. He felt that here was a man who wouldn't mind taking on the church hierarchy.

Barrett opened his heart to the northerner with the tightly clipped steelgrey hair and dark glasses, dressed in blue denim with a bright red t-shirt. "A red rag to the papal bull," Pat laughed despite the hurt to his dry lips. He told his life story from the beginning, the continuous challenge to authority in Maynooth, his work with the handicapped and mentally ill, his efforts to change attitudes to unmarried mothers, how he had provided single pregnant girls with a home when they were afraid to face their parents. Without naming names he told of Madeleine, of Joan, of Teresa and the love that had formed between them, how they had raised Jennie together until Teresa could take no more and had left him.

"It all sounds as if I'm just blowing my own trumpet." Barrett was embarrassed to find he was talking so much about himself.

"There is nothing wrong in telling it how it is. That, all the same, is the truth. You have left your mark on life. That is nothing to be ashamed of or embarrassed about. And where is your loved one, if I can put it like that, now?"

"Teresa? Down at home with her mother."

"You miss her an awful lot?"

"I thought that was obvious."

"Teresa's leaving you had a lot to do with your hunger-strike?"

"Of course it had. If she had stayed I would have had no problem with celibacy. We were married in everything but name as far as I was concerned."

"You would say then that her leaving you is the real reason for your hunger-strike?"

"You could put it like that...Indirectly, yes. It was Teresa's leaving that really put me thinking of what that stupid celibacy law is doing to the church."

"In other words if she had not left you would not be on hunger-strike. That is what I am trying to find out."

"It's not as simple as that, not as black and white as that..." Pat Barrett felt that this constant questioning was tiring him out. "I don't know what I am trying to say."

"I just have one or two more questions. Sorry for the hassle, but you understand that I do not want to misquote you or put words in your mouth."

"I appreciate that. If I had a drink I would be better. My mouth, my lips are all dry."

"I'm very sorry." Johnson stood up and reached for the jug beside the bed. "Where is the tap?"

"There will be no need for the hunger-strike if I drink tap water. It would be like taking poison. The sewer runs over beside the lake and seeps in some places. There is a bucket of water with muslin on top of it in the kitchen. The women bring me water from the well."

"If Teresa were to come back to you..." The journalist tried another question when Barrett had wet his mouth. "Would you give up the hunger-strike?"

"That does not arise. She has made her decision."

"Suppose she were to send a message through me..."

"If things were back to the way they used to be," Pat said wistfully.

"You would not be in danger of death?"

"Not from hunger anyway." Johnson ignored his attempt at a joke.

"Does Teresa know that?"

"I don't know what she knows or what she doesn't know. We have had no communication since she left. That's the way she wanted it."

"You think that she is willing to let you die?"

"Have I lost my marbles, or are we talking about the same person at all? Of course Teresa would not want me to die, but I'm sure she would respect my decisions as I would respect hers." Barrett was getting impatient and not a little angry. "Teresa had left before I decided to do this. It was not to hurt her or blackmail her that I went on hunger-strike, but to make sure the likes of this would not happen to any other woman or any other priest."

"Have you been psychologically assessed?"

"Am I mad you mean?" Barrett sounded flabbergasted. "Maybe I am."

"You seem somewhat naive to me. Don't get me wrong. That is not necessarily a bad thing. I mean naive in the sense that your...the founder of your religion was naive. Idealistically naive. Not streetwise enough for this world, and particularly for the hierarchy of you own faith."

"This seems to the one thing they do not have an answer to."

"I wouldn't be too sure of that."

"I wouldn't pretend to be sure of anything." Pat Barrett said in a low voice, almost absent-mindedly.

"Not even about your God?"

"Least of all about that. I am and I'm not, I suppose."

"A good Irish answer." Johnson held out his hand

and shook what seemed like a handful of bones in a plastic glove.

❦

Bishop Thomas Doherty tried to pray. Praying was hell, he thought. Not slipping a beads through his fingers and repeating the mantra like rhythms of the rosary. That he often found consoling, but talking straight to God, that was prayer of a different colour. Not that there was any point in being anything but straight with God. After all you couldn't pull the wool over the eyes of someone that knew everything. But what was he to say? God knew already what his dilemma was. He did not know what to do in the case of Pat Barrett.

The bishop knew that there were some problems that were unsolvable no matter what anyone did. This might be one of those insofar as Pat Barrett seemed to have them all over a barrel. To suspend him would probably strengthen his resolve to carry on his strike to the bitter end. To do nothing would seem like a sin of omission. He could not do more than his best. He would have to carry on trying to find an acceptable solution. If he failed, at least it would not be for want of trying.

He decided to put it all in the hands of God. It seemed strange that a bishop could almost overlook, forget about God. But that was what happened when he tried to bear the burden on his own. "Carry this load for me, Lord," he prayed. It worked too. Maybe it was just psychological, but it did take a weight off his mind to think that he was not alone in this. He remembered the old Isaiahan name for Jesus,

Emmanuel, God with us. Doherty repeated it a few times, "Emmanuel," "God with us." It helped relieve some of the pressure.

He resolved to visit Pat Barrett again within a couple of days, to talk it all over with him again, suss out how he was now after nearly six weeks on hunger-strike. Another couple of weeks and it would be getting too late. Mind or body could only take so much. He would begin to drift into and out of consciousness, be incapable of making a decision.

That might be where the best hope of beating the strike lay, in having his next of kin allow him to be fed intravenously when he became unconscious. He would have to speak with Pat's mother about it, a delicate matter. But that was how some of the northern hunger-strikers had been saved in the early eighties. He would get his secretary, Anthony Cosgrave to check it out. After all the man had a string of degrees in both canon and civil law. There was hardly a winter that he did not add to his list of degrees. This would give him an opportunity to make some real use out of what Doherty jokingly referred to as his hobby.

It had happened in the north that when hunger-strikers lost consciousness next of kin had allowed them to be fed, if they had not made a will or statement specifically forbidding it. Maybe Pat's mother could sign him that power so that he could intervene at any time to save her son. It seemed only a matter of time now until he would have to be cared for in hospital anyway. This would be one step, a small step towards avoiding the tragedy of Barrett's death. That too could be no more than a temporary respite. If the man wanted to die there was no way of stopping him.

Thomas Doherty rose from his prie-dieu to answer the phone. He felt that the call must be important or Cosgrave would not have him disturbed. His secretary wanted to know would he be willing to meet Eugene Johnson, the journalist, who had him pestered for an interview since morning. "Will I tell him that you're still at that conference?"

"He knows as well as we do that that is the equivalent of the two finger sign. It might be better not to rub that fellow up the wrong way. Tell him that I will grant him an interview in a couple of days, but that I want to have discussions with the nuncio and with Pat Barrett first. That should give us a little respite from the bastard."

"He's a sneaky one, that fellow."

"No better man than yourself to sing dumb out loud, Anthony. And that's a compliment. Only for you that media crowd would have me crucified."

❦

After leaving Pat Barrett Eugene Johnson decided to drop into the nearest bar to guage the level of local support for the priest's hunger-strike, and to pick up a couple of quotable quotes from the local worthies. He ordered a pint from Bartley and sat on a high stool talking about the weather and what kind of a tourist season they were having. He sensed that the men at the fire were listening carefully to the conversation, so he avoided any mention of what had brought him to the area.

Bartley excused himself after a while, saying that his dinner was waiting for him in the kitchen. "If you need me, give a blast on the old bell there."

"You couldn't do that in many places. I might have a couple of bottles of whiskey knocked off before you came back."

"You wouldn't do anything unknownst to the lads there." Bartley laughed. "My customers keep an eye out for me."

"Bartley there would sense from forty yards if a butterfly landed on the top of a whiskey bottle, not to speak of someone drinking or stealing one." Neddy John Tom raised his own almost empty pint glass in salute to the stranger as he spoke. But if the man with the dark glasses noticed the state of his glass he did nothing about it.

"Ye're alright there lads until I come back?" Bartley knew that the locals were in need of a refill and did not want to be called back in the middle of his dinner.

"Alright for the present, Bartley." Neddy was stoking up his pipe. "We'll be having a puff of tobacco while you're away. We don't want to disturb the spare ribs and cabbage. The smell would give anyone an appetite."

"Do you think will Donegal do any good in the Ulster championship this year?" Dara Nóra, knowing that the stranger had a northern accent tried to spin out a bait that might discover who he was or what brought him to the area. The man on the high stool didn't rise to the bait.

"Derry are usually near or near enough," Tomeen Mac Nicholl said, "though there isn't any of them has the same go in them as Down."

"Armagh had a good team a couple of years ago…" They would soon have named half the counties in Ulster, and your man hadn't budged. There wasn't a man in Ireland wouldn't stand up for his own county. Maybe this fellow was from the other side of the fence.

"I was in Donegal myself once," Cóilín a' Phortaigh said, "and in Tirconnell as well." He was confusing the two Irish names for the one county.

"You were not, Cóil?" Neddy faked wonderment even though Cóilín had told him a hundred times of the tour the priest had brought him on the previous year.

"Father Pat, the poor man that brought me." The journalist picked up his ears at the mention of the priest, but it had nothing to do with the hunger-strike, just some local idea of a joke.

"And how did you like Tirconnell, Cóil?" Neddy asked, knowing the answer better than himself.

"A grand place, but I preferred Donegal. It has this church built with red stones in it, and a big round chimney at the side of it."

"You were in Donegal town alright, Cóil." Dara Nóra said. "I've seen that chapel, out the road for Letterkenny."

"And what kind of a town is Tirconnell, Cóil?" Neddy was dying to hear his answer again.

"Sure it's not a town at all, Neddy, but a country, like the country around here, bog and mountain the most of it, and a lot of sea all around it, with big waves even in the summer. A lot of people does be drowned in it."

"The sea claims her own."

"It does, Dara, the Lord have mercy on them all." Cóilín removed his cap in respect for the dead.

Because there was no reference to the hunger-strike, Eugene Johnson asked, "Did I hear something about your priest here on the radio?"

"You could have and all," Neddy told him. "He has been known to give those little talks early in the morning, religious talks like, though I'm seldom awake myself in time to hear them. If the head is needing a cure in the morning, religion isn't always the first thing you want to hear either. That's what's so good about Saturday evening Mass for Sunday, if you get me. You don't have to listen to the religion too early in the day, when the head isn't clear like. You know yourself. I'm sure that I don't need to tell you about drink, or religion either for that matter. They seem to take it more serious in your part of the country, if you pardon me saying so, than we do down here."

"It must be taken seriously enough if a man is prepared to go on hunger-strike on a point of principle. I'm sure we're talking about the same man." Neddy ignored his reply.

"Would you be a manager yourself back in one of them factories on the new road?" he asked to change the subject. "Or are you just touring around?"

"Well, I travel a lot."

"Did I ever tell you about the Kerryman that came in here last year, or was it the year before?"

"It's unlikely that you told me." Johnson gave a half embarrassed laugh. "After all we never met until a half an hour ago."

"And you are very welcome to our parts." Neddy shook his hand. "Pleased to meet you." Spittle and porter froth that had accumulated around Neddy's lips sprayed Johnson in the face when he was up close. Using his own drink as an excuse he turned towards the counter, sipped his whiskey and said "You were telling me about the Kerryman."

"The Kerryman was on holidays below in one of them chalets that Bartley here rents out to strangers and tourists like. You could be staying in one of them yourself for all I know?"

"I'm just passing through, or I was, until your story started."

"He was like a young calf that you'd let out of the barn for the first time."

"The Kerryman?"

"You would think that he was never away from home before, but he was, you know. Himself and the wife used to go to Spain on their holidays year after year, until they got fed up baking their bellies in the sun. "Why don't we bring the children with us next year," he asked the missus on the beach one day, "and get a little houseen up in the west of Ireland for the holidays?" And that's what they did. They came here."

"That's the story of the Kerryman?"

"What's your hurry, man? Sure I'm only starting. But to make a long story short in case you are in a hurry. Our friend used to join us here for a few pints in the evening. A decent man he was, not afraid to put his hand in his pocket. But sure maybe he had plenty of it. He was a big farmer when he was at home. That was what he really enjoyed about around here. He didn't have to be up at five in the morning to have to start milking cows." Neddy pushed up close to Eugene Johnson, and elbowing him in the ribs in what he considered a friendly fashion, gave him another full frontal blast of stale Guinness. "You know how a Kerryman talks? They do say 'Ooo' instead of 'you.' He was telling us one day how much he enjoyed Bartley's chalet, and not having to get up in the morning to milk the cows. 'Ooo can do anything Ooo fuckin' like in the mornin' he said. 'Ooo can turn over and ride de wife if Ooo want. Ooo don't have to milk any fuckin cow or nothing.'" Everyone laughed except Johnson. He knew now that the men were far cuter than they pretended. They were playing games with him.

"Ooo could do worse than ride de wife," Tomeen tried to make the joke last.

"If Ooo had one." Dara Nóra reminded him.

"You do a lot of travelling yourself you said?" Neddy draped his arm across the journalist's shoulder.

"It's part of my job."

"Travelling on bad roads too, I might say," Dara said. "Are they as bad anywhere else as they are around here?"

"I'd say myself Cavan has the worst roads in the country." Johnson shrugged off Neddy's attentions and stood in the middle of the floor, speaking directly to Dara, whom he now regarded as the only one of the group that appeared half sensible.

"You must be staying locally?" Neddy was inquisitive again. "I didn't notice any car parked at the front when I was out at *teach an asail* as they call the asshouse around here."

"I came by taxi. It should be here to collect me soon."

"A taxi!" Neddy gave a gasp of amazement. "By God and you must have your money made, going here and there in a taxi."

"I'll bet anything," Tomeen said, "that you are a TD or a government minister."

"What kind of an *amadán* are you, Tomeen?" Neddy asked. "Wouldn't a government minister have his own Mercedes Benz and an armed detective to drive him?"

"Were you ever in Donegal or in Tirconnell,

yourself, sir?" Cóilín had awoken from a doze by the fire. Johnson ignored him. These old men disgusted him. He could not wait for the arrival of his taxi.

"I don't know, Cóilín," Neddy said, "but I think our man here is a biteen deaf."

❦

"You should call an emergency meeting of the community council." Pádraig Dara Nóra had scarcely sat into his headmaster's car before he was demanding a meeting. They travelled together to school, alternating cars. It was not that they had far to go, more something that had become a habit since one of the recurring oil crises of the previous decade.

"And what do we need the emergency meeting for?" Seán Donlon was tired of meetings, school meetings, meetings with education department officials, GAA, community council. There was a time when he had enjoyed them, but not since he had been made chairman.

"Didn't we complete the agenda at the monthly meeting?"

"You know as well as I do, Seán, that I'm talking about exceptional circumstances. It's not every day the local curate is on hunger-strike."

"What can we do about it? I'd leave that one to the church to sort out."

"But we're supposed to be the church. That's what they say anyway when it suits them, that it's not just the Pope and the bishops. We could find out if the bishop has agreed to intervene."

"He has."

"He has agreed, or he has intervened?"

"He is doing everything in his power to sort the whole mess out. I have no doubt but that he thinks of nothing else from morning till night."

"There's a big gap between thinking and doing. I think the community council should demand a meeting with the bishop."

"There is far too much demanding going on already. Demanding an end to celibacy. Demanding an end to the hunger-strike. Diplomacy is what is needed, not demanding."

"Next thing he'll be dead and everyone will be asking why we didn't do this or do that."

"Why don't you go to the bishop yourself?" Donlon was becoming impatient.

"It would be better if it came from the whole council, the representatives of the local people."

"I can't see what good it would do. The people themselves are divided on the issue."

"We might come to some conclusion if we had a meeting."

"The regular monthly meeting of the community council will take place as usual on the first Monday of the month." Sean Donlon spoke slowly and deliberately through his teeth as the anger arose inside him. "According to our constitution."

"The same constitution allows for an emergency meeting at any time, at the request of the chairperson or half the elected members."

"I am aware of the rules, Pádraig, and as chairman I see no need for a meeting at this time. I can only see it doing more harm than good. It would draw reporters like flies to a dungheap, split the community even more."

"Ah, dictators are all the same..." Pádraig's

throwaway remark incensed his headmaster. He braked suddenly, pulling in to the left hand side of the road at the same time. Only his safety belt kept Pádraig Dara Nóra from crashing his head against the front window.

"What the hell?" But Seán was not there to answer. He had got out, walked around the car, opened the door on Pádraig's side and demanded—"Out!"

"What has got into you?"

"I don't have to take insults in my own car."

"Insults. What insults?"

"You called me a dictator."

"You weren't prepared to call a meeting that is badly needed."

"There is more to committees and councils than talk, and all you ever do is talk and complain and run people down. There is never much sight of you when there is a protest to be made or a delegation to be sent someplace. Someone not worth two fucks himself isn't going to call me a dictator." He closed the door with a bang, got in his own side of the car and drove on. Pádraig didn't dare open his mouth. He had never known the older man to get angry or use bad language before.

"Bring your own car tomorrow," the headmaster said gruffly as he let Pádraig off at his father's gate.

༄

Teresa Carter was looking forward greatly to her new life in the university. It pleased her mother to see her in such good form, the weight of depression that had hung over her all summer lifted. "There'll be no stopping you at all when you meet some nice fellow..."

She knew immediately that she had said the wrong thing.

"There's a far better chance of you falling in love than me, mam."

"Sorry. I'm always putting my big foot in it, but you seem so much happier in yourself since you came back from the city."

"I was so nervous, but everything worked out alright. So far."

"You won't have any problems. You were always good at school."

"I seem to have lost confidence or something, to expect everything to be so hard. I was dreading just going in to sort things out in the university, and sure there was no problem at all when I got there."

"I suppose everyone else is just as nervous."

"I doubt it. Sure for most of them it's just changing from one school to another. I have not stood in a school for four years."

"People surely don't forget what they have learned. If they do what good is any school?"

"The best thing about university is that you can choose a few of your best subjects. I wouldn't like to have to face maths after four years."

"You'll be alright." Her mother gently patted her hand. They had sat long over dinner, as if each wanted the good feeling between them to last. They had not always got on well.

"I'm going to miss Jennie so much."

"You will only be away four nights any week, and it's not as if she does not know me."

"It's not that, mam. I know you will look after her better than myself."

"I'll do my best."

"You have plenty of practice, anyway, after rearing seven of us."

"The time goes so fast. The full of the house today. All gone tomorrow."

"Sure Noel is only a couple of hundred yards over the road."

"The house was quiet all the same until yourself and Jennie came back."

"You'll be driven out of your mind with her constant questioning."

"It's better than the loneliness any day."

"I don't know how it was I couldn't bring myself to tell you about Jennie at the beginning." Teresa was fondling her mother's hand almost absent-mindedly as she spoke.

"There were so many of ye in it, like steps of stairs, that I didn't have time to get to know each of ye as well as I should when ye were growing up. And with your father gone..."

"You were father and mother to us. You certainly provided well."

"I suppose that I was too hard on ye. But I felt that manners and discipline were so important. Especially when there was not a man in the house."

"Sure they are important too." Teresa smiled. "You weren't that bad."

"Didn't you as much as say that you were afraid of me, that you couldn't tell me about Jennie?"

"I wasn't afraid in the sense that I thought you would beat me, but that I would be letting you down after all your efforts to rear us well."

"Every father and mother should get a second chance. When they have their family reared they should be let start again so that they could do it all differently, not make the same mistakes again. That's the best about being a grandmother. I'm looking forward to minding Jennie, to be more relaxed than I was with ye."

"You did alright with us. I hope that you don't have anything too new in mind." Teresa was really enjoying their conversation, woman to woman more than mother to daughter. She hoped that Jennie, who had lain on the couch after her dinner would snooze a while longer.

"I wouldn't take as much notice of what Popes or bishops said anyway," her mother mused.

"You are talking about contraception?"

"Among other things."

"Some of us wouldn't be in it at all, so. Are you sorry you had such a big family?"

"It's not as if I didn't care about each and every one of you. But I would like to have had more time with your father."

"If you spent much more time with him you would have fourteen instead of seven." They laughed heartily, unused to joking with each other about such matters.

"I meant time together without children under our feet all the time. Other people get that chance when their children are reared."

"Poor dad...He went very quick."

"Sometimes I wonder is there a God at all."

"Mam...Of all the people in the world...You have more faith than anyone I know."

"For all the good it did me. My husband swept away from me in his prime."

"I never thought I'd see the day you would question God."

"God forgive me. It's not that I don't believe, but

I could do without some of the crosses."

"Like Jennie and me?" Teresa asked gently.

"Jennie is a blessing," her mother said, and with a slow smile, "whatever about you."

"I suppose I have drawn a lot of talk..." Teresa thought there was more in what her mother said than just a joke. "An unmarried mother, Pat, everything."

"Talk never put a bite in anyone's mouth. I wish I was as free as you when I was your age."

"But you had a grand simple life, a home of your own, a man that loved you."

"Can you keep a secret?"

"Try me...Of course I can." Teresa was afraid her mother would change her mind and not tell whatever it was.

"I was pregnant when I married your father."

"Sure I knew that."

"You knew?"

"It doesn't take a detective to count the months between the date of your wedding anniversary and Noel's birthday. Unless he was four months premature."

"And do they all know?"

"You're blushing, mam. Of course they know. It's a long time since we worked that one out. Maybe Noel doesn't know though. We didn't like to say it to him."

"I told Noel myself."

"And didn't tell the rest of us?"

"Amn't I after telling you now?"

"And why didn't you tell the rest?"

"Maybe it was none of your business. Not until you had Jennie, maybe. So that you would know I understand what it is like to be single and pregnant."

"A pity you didn't tell me a couple of years ago."

"You were not always a great one to listen. I told Noel in case he would find out for himself and that it would hurt him. And there was something else. Maybe you know this too."

"How will I know until you say it?" Teresa gave a nervous laugh. "This is better than the telly. Next thing you will be telling me that I'm a changeling, that I was left by the fairies."

"You're yourself alright. I'm beginning to think you're more like me than any of them. Maybe we're too alike, and that's why we have not always got on."

"Is that the big secret?" Teresa looked disappointed.

"No." Her mother looked her straight in the eye. "But Noel is not your father's son."

"Noel? Whose is he? I don't know that I want to hear all this, mam. Did dad know?"

"Of course he knew."

"You were two timing...?"

"I was not. I hardly knew your father when we married. It was arranged when my parents found out I was pregnant."

"And they didn't want you to marry Noel's father?"

"He was married already."

"Jesus. We all thought butter wouldn't have melted in your mouth."

"You don't have to take the holy name in vain."

"After what I'm hearing?"

"It was the time they were putting in the electricity. We got it later than most because the Gleann was so out of the way. There was a big gang of men on the scheme, most of them local, but the fellow in charge was from the city."

"And that was how you met your handsome stranger?"

"We used to make tea for them, and there were house dances in the evenings."

"And no one said he was married?"

"I doubt if they knew. Anyway it was the best thing ever happened to me in a way or I would never have met your father."

"And you didn't meet him until the day you got married? Like buying a pig in a bag?"

"I wouldn't put it quite like that. We met about a month before the wedding."

"When the bargain was being made?"

"You could call it that. That's the way things were done at the time, and that's not forty years ago." Mary Carter laughed. "You are right about the bargain. I never thought of it like that. It was actually at the fair that it was all arranged, the *cleamhnas*."

"They didn't have you at the fair?"

"They didn't. There was no need to look at my teeth and vet me to see what age I was. They knew I was young. Too young. Young enough to be foolish. Young enough to have a houseful of children. And your father got a bargain in his own way. He was a bachelor, getting on a bit. A good bargain, a young wife, even if she did have a bun in her oven."

"And did you love the other man?"

"I thought I did. Until he found out that I was pregnant. Until I found out that he was married."

"And did it take you long to fall in love with Dad, as you obviously did?"

"I suppose that when I married him I accepted that it was my duty to love him. As it turned out he was the easiest man in the world to love. He expected nothing at all from life. He looked on everything good as a grace from God."

"I find it hard to understand how you could love one man today, another tomorrow."

"Isn't it the same in your own case," her mother said gently. "Jennie's father, and Pat?"

"Maybe you're right, that we're more alike than I ever thought. It's just that I have to go a step further, to lose both of them."

"I lost a man too, to death, but for what it's worth, I don't think Pat is going to die."

"I have lost him anyway, death or no death. I have let him go, because we weren't going anywhere." Teresa surprised herself that she was so matter of fact, unsentimental about it.

Their intimacy was interrupted by a loud knocking on the front door.

"I'll get it," Teresa stood up.

"Leave it be." Her mother sensed some kind of threat.

"Maybe Pat has..."

"Wait here." Mary Carter went to the front door but did not open it. "Who is it?"

"My name is Eugene Johnson," a northern accent replied. "I'm a journalist. I would like the opportunity to have a few words with Teresa Carter. Sorry I'm so late. I found it hard to find the house."

"She is not here."

"Are you her mother?"

"The guards said to ring them if there were strangers around at night."

"I have an ID card."

"You can show it to the sergeant. Wait until I ring them."

"Leave it." Teresa and her mother watched from the sitting room window as a taxi drove away.

❦

His bishop, Thomas Doherty was sitting by Pat Barrett's bed when he awoke. In the hazy time between sleeping and waking it took the priest a couple of moments to work out if he was dreaming or if the bishop was really there. There had been so many and such strange dreams lately that he was not sure about his hold on reality. He was weak. His eyes were sore and even with the curtains closed the muted light of a yellow bulb made them hurt. His mouth was dry and tasted like he had eaten manure. He could hardly move a limb. He wished the bishop would just go away, let him sleep, at least pretend he was asleep. But somewhere deep down in him the respect for authority, or at least for Doherty the man, had the upper hand.

"You're welcome," he muttered from between dry lips.

"How are you, Pat?" The bishop laid a hand over Pat's when he saw that he was about to try to shake hands with him. "Don't stir."

"Not too bad. How are you keeping yourself?"

"Keeping the best side out." There was what seemed to Pat like a strained silence. He felt it was no time for beating around bushes. "I suppose you're here to ask me to give up the strike."

"I just came to see you. As a friend."

"That's nice," Pat said with a hint of sarcasm. "You didn't bring the big stick with you so?"

"I don't think it would do much good at this point in time."

"Well, where's the carrot so?"

"No carrot either. Do it your own way, Pat."

"No word from Rome?"

"None, though the crocodile wants me to put my foot down."

"McIntosh? Do what you have to do, Tom. Say what you have to say for public consumption. At this stage I don't have very much to lose."

"I'm half tempted to go on hunger-strike along with you."

"Pull my other leg, if there's anything left to pull. One is enough. One person is too much to be starving himself to death."

"It would be worth it to stick one to that fecker of a nuncio."

"They might take a bit of notice of a bishop on hunger-strike."

"No way. The day Rome surrenders on one like this, that's the day Rome is finished."

"Rome was not finished in a day," Pat Barrett tried to joke.

"Look at it from the Pope's point of view, Pat. If he were to give in under pressure. If he were to give in without pressure, even, he would have a schism on his hands. I'll have you know that there are millions of Catholics out there that want a celibate clergy."

"It's better that one man should die, than for the rock of Peter to perish." Barrett mixed his biblical quotations deliberately. He felt lightheaded. He didn't give a damn, he felt at that very moment what any pope or bishop said. He felt a sense of power, almost, an arrogant sense of anarchy. He had them eating out of his hand, if only for a couple of weeks.

"I'm not saying that every clergyman succeeds in living a chaste life all the time," Thomas Doherty went on, only to be rudely interrupted by his priest.

"Did you ever have the ride yourself, Tom?" He seemed taken aback for a moment.

"Now that you mention it, Pat, I didn't." The bishop recovered his composure quickly.

"There's some that calls it an overrated pastime."

"And do they exaggerate?" Doherty decided that it was better join them if you couldn't beat them.

"It's not for nothing that thy call you a cute hoor, Tom. Does anything ever knock you out of your stride?"

"You do, for one. You have fairly put me through the hoops in the last couple of months." It was now Barrett's turn to be taken aback. "I'm sorry."

"Maybe you didn't think it through enough, Pat. Maybe you didn't think of what your lousy strike is doing to other people, to people who love you, to your mother, to the people of the parish here, to me, to the priests of the diocese, to the woman and child you claim to love. Think about it, Pat. Think about it hard. They say a deathbed is as good a place as any for an examination of conscience."

"For a man that didn't bring the big stick, you're laying it on heavy."

"I didn't come here to upset you, Pat, but those things needed to be said. There's more to life than sex or celibacy. The world doesn't revolve around your prick, or mine for that matter."

"I never suggested that it did." Pat Barrett said quietly.

"It's important to see the other side too, that there are thousands of priests out there who live by the rules, who do not always succeed, but they do make strong efforts to live chaste celibate lives."

"A bottle replacing the woman in many cases. Half

of them are alcoholics."

"I'm not the judge. OK, I see the big cars, the foreign holidays, people's pathetic efforts, you might think to fill an emptiness in their lives. But through and through they try to live up to the vows they have taken. I appreciate, admire, am inspired by that, despite the failures. It is after all a human, sinful church."

"I suppose you think I'm completely out of my mind?"

"You're not, Pat, but you're using a sledgehammer to kill a fly. OK, I know how this celibacy thing weighs heavily on the younger priests."

"It doesn't effect the oldtimer at all?" Despite the earlier exchanges there was a glint of humour in Barrett's eye. "I suppose that when a man gets the mitre, the old concupiscence as it used to be called, dries up."

"Not as long as a man lives."

"It could happen a bishop?"

"Should might be the operative word." Thomas Doherty was smiling again.

"Are you trying to tell me that you're gone past it?"

"I heard an old missioner tell a story once," the bishop said. An old parish priest invited his pals to supper the following Friday. He had reached the venerable age of ninety and felt that he had at last got the upper hand on what you called concupiscence. It was to celebrate this momentous success that he was calling his friends together. On the Thursday night he sent each of them a telegram—"supper indefinitely postponed."

"That was a good one, talking about the upper hand in that context."

"You haven't lost your mind yet, the dirty part of it anyway."

"There are times I think I have. I cannot imagine how someone like Bobby Sands could keep on writing poetry almost until the end, it seems."

"How much of it did he really do? How much of it was propaganda?"

"I would say he did it alright. I have always despised the IRA, but that does not prevent me admiring Sands and his colleagues. They were brave men."

"They were used."

"They decided themselves to do it. They felt it better to die than put up with their conditions."

"Their protests did more harm than good in the long run."

"There are times that no other method works. I often felt at the end of the seventies that it was a pity some or all of the bishops had not gone on hunger-strike."

"The bishops?" Thomas Doherty raised his eyebrows in wonder.

"If they had done so between the deaths of Frank Stagg and Michael Gaughan and the other ten, they could have had a major effect on putting an end to violence."

"On hunger-strike for what?"

"For an end to violence. For a ceasefire."

"When they took no heed of Pope John Paul in Drogheda. On his bended knees..."

"It's easy go on your knees. It's not easy to put your life on the line. I'm telling you there would be notice taken if a group of bishops went on hunger-strike. Look at the amount of pressure that even a priesteen on a fast gets."

"I wouldn't like to be the one to suggest it at a meeting of the hierarchy in Maynooth. Anyway it's just another form of violence—against the self." Pat Barrett ignored the bishop's barb about violence. "Once the ten were dead in the H-block it was too late to use that as a weapon," he said.

"In a purely tactical sense you would think that was the time it would be strongest." The bishop was prepared to debate the point even though the whole idea was anathema to him. "Keep talking," he told himself. It was as if he was dealing with someone holding hostages, or ready to jump off a building. The priest stuck to his argument;

"At that stage the IRA would only have said—'You took no notice of our men, why should we heed you? Fuck ye...'"

"That would be nothing new from them. Every bomb and bullet of theirs says the same thing—'Fuck you.' Anyway there was less notice taken of Gaughan and Stagg than the other ten up north."

"There was not much notice taken of their demands, but a lot of notice was taken of them as martyrs. Not many more have had a ton of concrete poured over them to keep their wasted bodies from escaping the grave. There was an atmosphere there at the time that the hierarchy could have used in the peace process. They could have said—'If you want us to heed your martyrs, give our sacrifice the same respect, because we too are prepared to suffer.' But when have you seen bishops make any more than a paper stand about anything, make a stand about anything if it comes to that, except sex."

"That's a wild exaggeration, and not a little ironic from a man putting his life on the line for something not unconnected with sex. The hierarchy have taken many stands. We have gone against the popular tide more often than not."

"You have gone against the grain more often than against the tide. You seem to spend most of your time defending the indefensible."

"It might look that way to people who do not see things from our point of view."

"If you spent as much time preaching the gospel as you do condemning condoms, even though they are the only real protection against AIDS." Barrett tried to get in as many barbs as possible. He was still hurt by Doherty's earlier remarks which had stung him to the marrow.

"I think the same condoms are suspiciously like red herrings in the present circumstances." The bishop felt more at ease now, felt he might be winning the argument at last.

"Every one of the hierarchy should put a condom on the end of his crozier. They wouldn't make as much noise that way." Doherty laughed easily even though the joke was not new.

"You wouldn't think, Pat, that you have done enough at this stage to highlight the celibacy thing?"

"If I were to give up now, it would look as if it was hypocritical all along."

"Would you not think that your death could do more harm than good? What about the people of the parish here, who have great *meas* on you, great respect for you?"

"That will hardly change if I follow my conscience, do what I think is right."

"Not that everyone is a hundred percent behind you. I get letters..."

"No need to spell out who from."

"I cannot tell you that."

"If I mentioned a certain teacher in the secondary school, would I be far off the mark?"

"Private, personal, confidential letters."

"I don't know what turned him against me in the first place. A roasting I gave him on the football field, maybe. He never agreed with anything I said or proposed at a public meeting. That fellow is against everything."

"We all rub people the wrong way now and again, more often than not without intending it. They turn against us sometimes, not because of anything we have done. A belting they got from some other member of the clergy, maybe..."

"Are there many other than the said Pádraig complaining about me?"

"I never mentioned any Pádraig."

"Probably writes under a false name."

"This is beginning to sound very like paranoia, Pat. If you have something against this fellow, it might be time to clear your conscience." The bishop was determined to remind Barrett of his impending death as often and in as many ways as he could. He had heard it said that death has a great way of concentrating the mind, but this man's mind seemed to be concentrated on everything except finding a way out of his dilemma. "Is it worth leaving this world with a set on this particular fellow? For a man that used have a reputation of being broadminded..."

"I don't know, Tom." Pat Barrett seemed to sink back in the pillows as if he had somehow lost the will to live. "I don't know anything about anything any more. When a person goes this far it is so hard to turn back." The bishop sensed a chink in his armour. It was time to be kind. "It's not easy for anyone to give an inch in matters like this, not easy for a pope or a bishop either."

"They don't have death staring them in the face."

"You don't either, except by your own choice. Nobody wants to lose face, Pat, but there is always a middle way if people are prepared to seek it, if they have the will to pursue it."

"This is as black and white a situation as you can get, in my opinion. If there is a middle way, let's hear it. What do you see as the compromise position, this middle way?"

"There is little point in me suggesting anything, if you are determined on martyrdom, Pat."

"I don't want to fucking die any more than you do." The vehemence of the reply surprised, but also pleased the bishop. "Now we're talking, Pat," he said.

"If we are, I haven't heard anything yet." Barrett's smile turned into a grin because his lips were sore. "What do you suggest as a way of getting me off this hook?"

"As I have said already there is no authority in the world that can be seen to surrender under pressure. If they do that is the end of their authority. But if the threat were taken away people might be able to do business..."

"I'll probably be dead before you get to the point." Despite his sarcasm, Barrett was interested. "What formula of words could possibly solve this? There is no way your crowd is going to give."

"My crowd, as you call us happen to be your crowd too, Pat. It's delicate, but even McIntosh would go along with it. He's a realist." Doherty spoke more quickly as if embarrassed. "It boils down to letting yourself and the er, girl live under the same roof, rear the child, et cetera. No questions asked. No detectives checking the beds."

"More hypocrisy. What's new, pussycat?" Barrett said resignedly. "Didn't we live like that already?"

"But there would be a formality about this, some sort of ceremony, commitment."

"A dry marriage..." The priest spoke scathingly. "Like the dry ride your friend, the priest psychologist recommended to us at the retreat last year. Everything goes almost except actually doing the job. That kind of hypocrisy is worse than having it off right on the quiet."

"You are making something sleazy out of something beautiful." The bishop was finding it hard to remain patient, but he couldn't afford to explode now that he had created an opening.

"All I'm trying to do Pat is to find an honourable way out of your dilemma. I don't mind what that way is except that it be honourable. I don't want to screw you, Pat, or I don't want to see you screwing the church."

"I accept that screwing is out anyway." There was a glint in Barrett's eye.

"It's in your own hands, Pat."

"I'll think over all we talked about. And Tom... I'd appreciate your blessing, and your prayers.

❧

Johnny McKay was still in hospital when the school reopened after the summer holidays. Darina had returned to work a fortnight earlier, but came home every weekend to see her father. The doctors said that he was steadily improving but that his recovery would take time.

Aisling Dara Nóra was back at school, but not only was she not speaking to Martina, she took every opportunity she could to give her a one fingered or two fingered salute, which in school language spelt respectively if not respectfully "up yours," "fuck off," or the latest salute, three fingers which meant "fuck off, in inverted commas." Martina felt that Aisling was probably spreading false rumours about her, because many of the other students seemed to be avoiding her.

On the other hand she felt that it might just be jealousy. She had got good marks in her Junior Certificate examination. She resolved to work hard for her two remaining years in school. If she was to do as well in the Leaving Certificate. She knew that she would have enough points to get into veterinary medicine, possibly the most difficult area in the universities to get a place in. It was not that she had changed her mind much about farmwork. She liked animals. There was a big difference between haymaking in the oldfashioned way on their small rocky farm and caring for animals in a hospital type situation. She intended to do so well that she wouldn't have to care who spoke to her and who didn't.

Inevitably Father Pat's hunger-strike took up a lot of time in religion class, arguments for and against, Sister Damien trying to be fair to both sides. Although into her forties Damien was the youngest nun on the staff. She had a reputation as a great fundraiser for charity, so much so that the picture of her meeting the Pope during an audience in Rome had become the source of one of the stories told about her. This picture, which hung inside the college entrance showed the pope holding Damien by both her hands as she talked animatedly to him. It had drawn the drywitted comment from Sean Donlon, the school principal— "The poor man was only trying to keep her hands out of his pockets."

For once Sister Damien had no difficulty in interesting her class in a subject usually described by them as "dead boring." While many of the pupils supported Pat Barrett's stance partly because he was the school chaplain and they liked him, others like Aisling, maybe reflecting the views of her brother, Pádraig, took a different line. "He should stick to the vows he took when he was ordained."

"A lot of people do a lot of things when they are young that they regret later," Martina said. The nun sensed the tension between the girls and tried to move on. But she could not ignore Aisling's raised hand. "I have a question about AIDS sister."

"Can we stick to the subject that is under discussion. We will come to that another day. I'm glad you brought it up, though, Aisling."

It was as they went up the boreen from where the school bus dropped them that Davoren said "A lot must think that TB is contagious. Hardly anyone is talking to me."

"I never thought of that," Martina said. "That explains it. They are keeping away from me too. I was wondering had I a bad smell, or something."

"Fuck them." Davoren sullenly kicked a small stone ahead of him.

"I'll tell Donlon about them."

"Stay away from him anyway." Davoren disliked the headmaster since he had wrongly accused him of smoking in the toilets.

"Don't say anything to mam. Let it blow over." As they approached the house, Spot, the dog came out to meet them, wagging not just his tail, but his whole body from side to side. Martina hugged him. Animals, she thought, were a lot nicer than people most of the time.

"You're very quiet this evening," their mother remarked when they were in the car on their way to see Johnny in hospital.

"It takes a while to get used to school again." Martina stretched and gave a pretend yawn. Davoren gave her the thumbs up sign when she peeked back at him. He suddenly became very animated, talking about everything and anything, in case Barbara would think there was something wrong if they were quiet.

It raised their spirits to find their father walking around the hospital corridor, full of good humour and chat. By the time they got back and started on their homework, they had almost forgotten the way their fellow pupils had treated them earlier in the day.

🍂

Eugene Johnson made a couple of more efforts to contact Teresa Carter for an interview. He came to the door of her mother's house in a hired car the morning after he had failed to speak to her.

"You're back again," Mary opened the door, and stood smiling, winding her hands together inside her apron. "It's hard to get rid of a bad thing."

"You don't know whether I'm good or bad until you talk to me."

"I'm talking to you now, and I'm telling you Teresa

is not at home."

"If I had given up every time I was fed that line..." Johnson said "Look. There could be something for her out of this..."

"Something to sell your dirty rag of a paper."

"I'm not after sensational stuff. I talked to Father Barrett. I have an appointment with Bishop Doherty. I just want to hear Teresa's view of the priest's hunger-strike from her own lips."

"Maybe she would know what you're talking about, but I don't."

"I would like to hear it from her own mouth."

"You will hear it from the sergeant's mouth if you don't go away." Mary Carter moved in behind her front door and closed it gently in his face.

Johnson went away but he did not leave the area. A phonecall to the social welfare office told him which day a single mother would be entitled to collect her allowance from the post office. She would have to leave the house sometime. He would stalk the area around the house as well as the church and post office until she showed up. He had a good idea that the post office was the best bet. A young single mother would hardly survive very long without her social welfare allowance.

It was a long day. He read every paper, local and national, listened to news after news on the radio, music, current affairs programmes. He was a man for the long haul. That was how he made his reputation as a dogged journalist that would not let go the bone that might make a good story. So what if he was unscrupulous, tough, mean? His stories got printed. Editors paid up. His was a hands-on journalism, not the sit on your arse and dawdle on your word processor journalism of the new breed of self opinionated "opinion formers' who spent their time defying one of the basic rules of logic, arguing from the particular to the general.

Johnson had the bones of his story written as he wanted to write it. What he wanted, waited for now was a little flesh for those bones, proof that he was there, that he got the quotes, took the pictures, whatever. He didn't want, didn't need some fancy photographer tagging along after him. He was no photographic genius but he took clear recognisable shots to help make his stories stand up. Saved money for the journals that way too. There were pictures of Barrett and Doherty on file all over the place. No one had seen or heard of the little heartbreaker that had caused all the trouble. While the "opinion formers' wrote the learned philosophical stuff about the morality of a hunger-strike, Eugene was out stalking the quarry for his scoop.

Must be an interesting girl, he thought. "I hope she talks. No one has ever really given the woman's side of the story in a situation like this." As he talked to himself he noticed in his mirror a woman and child coming slowly down the road, the woman walking at the child's pace, which he found unusual. In the city women seemed to either push their children in buggies or drag them along by the hand. It was nice to see someone who was not in a hurry.

This may or may not be Ms. Carter, he said to himself, but I'll bet that there are not too many single mothers' allowances to be collected in a rural backwater like this. He waited until the young woman he had seen approaching the post office had her business done.

"Teresa?" he said as he opened the car door quickly, and although she did not reply, he knew from her reaction that he was right. "A goodlooker too," he thought as he admired the pixie-cut black hair framing a darkeyed, big cheekboned face. She stood, dumbfounded, looking at him, recognising the accent, quivering with a sudden fright. Then she took herself in hand, reminded herself that she owed this fellow nothing, and decided to try and work the head on him. She put her hand to her mouth, indicating that she was dumb.

"You are Teresa Carter?" Johnson was surprised by her strange actions. Teresa made the same gesture, as Jennie stood, her head sideways, looking quizically at her.

"The man is talking to you, Mammy." Teresa shook her head, and put her hand up to her mouth again.

"You can talk. I know that you can talk." Johnson had not come across this trick previously. "You needn't be afraid. I just want to ask you a couple of simple questions." Teresa shook her head again, took Jennie's hand, and walked on down the road.

"Is he a bad man, Mammy. Is he the bogeyman?" Teresa nodded and hurried on.

"I'm no bogeyman." The journalist had heard the child's question. "I'm a friend of Pat Barrett's. I have a message from him for you."

Teresa stopped in the middle of the road. Maybe he was telling the truth. She doubted it. She turned again and walked away from Johnson, who shouted after her;

"He loved you. He still loves you. I know that, he told me." Teresa walked on.

"Two can play the deaf and dumb game," the journalist said to himself, trying to scribble in his note book and run after Jennie and her mother at the same time. When he caught up he handed Teresa the note, asking for a short interview, in words or writing. She turned over the page of the notebook, indicated that she wanted his pen and wrote something. Then she suddenly threw the pen and paper across the stone wall. He had a fair idea of what she had written as he clambered across the wall to retrieve his notepad and biro—"Go away and fuck yourself."

"And fuck you too," he shouted after her, even though he knew she was well out of earshot at this stage. He was mad with himself more than with her. he had left his camera in the car instead of photographing herself and her daughter, whether it was against her will or not. "Don't for a moment think you're finished with Eugene," he said through gritted teeth. "I'll be after you like a ferret after a rabbit."

❧

Seamus, Mickey and Macdara went into hard training again for the *currach* racing. Although they had taken two seconds and a third place in the races which move from one coastal village to another during the month of August, they had failed to finish in what they considered their rightful place, first. But now the big one was coming up, the champion of champions which would really decide which was the best crew in the west. Every team which had won a major race all summer was eligible, and as Seamus' crew had four wins to their credit, three in Connemara, and one in Dingle, they were in for "seaimpín na seaimpíní" the champion of champions to be decided at Trá an Dóilín, the coral strand at Carraroe.

"What has come over ye?" Seamus was angry because his companions seemed to be just going through the motions without spirit or style. "Whatever ye're thinking about it's not the race on Sunday week."

"You're not pulling so well yourself," Mickey said sourly. "Macdara and me were stroke for stroke there for a while, and you weren't pulling right with us at all."

"Come on and we'll have another go." Seamus tried to encourage them. Macdara reached for his oars, and Mickey for his fags. "It's no use," he said, spitting over the side of the canvas canoe.

"What's no use? What the fuck is wrong with ye?" Seamus could see his hopes for the championship slipping away.

"Everybody knows," Mickey said quietly, "but no one wants to say it."

"Everybody knows what. Come to the bloody point." Macdara rested on the oars.

"I'd be worried if I was in either of your shoes." Mickey was just as vague. "Thanks be to Christ I didn't have anything to do with either of them."

"What the hell is he talking about?" Macdara could only answer Seamus' question with a shrug of his shoulders.

"Bloody AIDS. That's what I'm talking about. That's what everyone is talking about, everyone except the ones that has it."

"You've lost me." Seamus spread his hands in a gesture of incomprehension.

"Don't the dogs in the street know that that's what

McKay brought back from the States." Mickey gave
wind to the latest rumour around the village. Macdara
and Seamus began to laugh, but the smiles seemed to
grind to a halt on their faces.

"Seafóid," Macdara said, but not without doubt.

"Who told you anyway?" Seamus asked Mickey
aggressively.

"Doesn't the whole country know that the man is
on his deathbed in the hospital."

"You're always exaggerating," Macdara said. "A
month ago you were telling us Father Pat was on his
last gasp and he's still alive."

"How do we know he's not eating on the quiet? I
heard the bishop gave out stink to him the last day. He
said he'd excommunicate him if he didn't give it up."

"What good would that do, Mickey, if he is dead
anyway?" Macdara wanted to know.

"It'll put him down to the pits of hell. Down he'll
be going anyway if he kills himself. I'm telling ye, the
man has brought a curse on this place with his carry
on. There was never AIDS or anything like that around
here before."

"Darina said he was improving." Seamus was more
interested in the health of his prospective father in law
than in the priest's problems."

"Jesus Christ almighty," Mickey said. "You hardly
expect his family to go around boasting about it."

"It's that TB he has." Macdara sounded surer than
he was.

"Do you expect anyone in the west of Ireland to
admit out loud that they have AIDS?" Mickey was
lighting another cigarette as he spoke. "Of course
they'll say that it's TB or cancer or leukaemia that they
have. From what I hear two out of every three that is

said to have cancer are suffering from AIDS," he said knowingly.

"But it's not supposed to be contagious?" Macdara was grasping at straws at this stage.

"What else would you expect them to say?" Mickey spoke as if he were an expert. "If it's not contagious how is it that they are so careful about it in the hospitals, masks and gloves and everything on them. I've seen a few programmes about it on the television. McKay will die roaring yet, if the ticker doesn't give out in the meantime."

"How could he pick it up even if he was in the States?" Seamus was worrying more and more about Darina and himself.

"How does anyone get it?" Mickey asked. "Didn't you hear about that American basketball player, Magic Johnson?"

"You're not trying to tell us Johnny McKay is gay?" Macdara unintentionally displayed his ignorance on the matter.

"Magic Johnson was no homo, either." Mickey said. "Anyone can get it."

"But Johnny McKay is a married man. He wouldn't be...Seamus did not know what to say. It was if the bottom was beginning to slowly fall out of his life and hopes."

"Married or single...When a man is lonely away from home." Mickey had all the answers, as far as he was concerned himself anyway.

"Fuck this for a crack, We're not going to do any good this evening." Seamus tightened his grip on his oars. "Let's go and get pissed."

❧

Dawn had barely broken when Eugene Johnson made his way to the top of the hill which rose almost as sheer as a cliff a couple of hundred yards to the south west of Carter's house. He had his binoculars and camera, a small flask of whiskey and some chocolate. Teresa did not appear at all during the day. Her mother came out the back door a couple of times to feed the hens and the geese, the little girl hovering around her skirts, or running when a goose stretched out a long neck to hiss at her. Johnson had built himself a rough stone seat behind a rambling limestone wall. He could sit all day and observe the house through a hole between the stones of the wall.

About midday a thick wetting mist drifted in from the Atlantic and drenched him to the skin. Although the forecast had promised high pressure and sunshine in many areas, it had warned of fog and mist in some coastal places if the sun failed to burn through. It was just his luck. For a man who claimed not to believe in anything he was deeply superstitious. "Third time lucky," he said to himself. "I lost her yesterday. I lost her today. I'll get the bitch tomorrow." He decided to go back to his hotel, have a hot bath and a whiskey to avoid catching a cold. He would come better prepared the following day.

Next morning he bought an oilskin outfit in the nearest town. He took his time getting to his vantage point, as there was still a fog. The grey limestone all around depressed him. He couldn't understand what beauty people saw in it. And yet they were prepared to mount campaigns to prevent the progress represented by interpretive centres, and preserve the place as a bird sanctuary. What birds? The only one he had seen was a hawk hovering in search of mice or something. He liked the hawk, a bird of prey waiting to pounce.

The sun burned through the fog in mid morning, clearing the top of the hill first and then quickly burning off the white down that drifted below him. The day was a complete contrast to the previous one. The oilskins were quickly discarded, followed by his jacket, shirt and vest. He remembered having heard somewhere that limestone is one of the warmest of rocks, and he had no difficulty believing it. There seemed to be fumes of heat rising from the stone, as much warmth coming from below as from the sun overhead. To pass the time he took some pictures of the house. At least he would have that to show if he failed to get the girl. The morning drifted into afternoon, with even the hens apparently unfed, apart from their picking around the yard.

A sudden flutter of wings told Johnson that the hawk was back and in action. It had swooped on something, apparently missed, because it rose again quickly, only to be chased by two smaller black looking birds. This fascinated him, David and Goliath stuff, even if there were two Davids. He clicked a series of pictures before the little birds returned to seemingly settle in a clump of blackberry brambles. All was quiet again. Or was it?

They were a long way away from him but the little girl's voice carried in the clear air. She was walking with her mother along the little boreen that led from the back of the house towards the sea. The journalist could not believe his luck. He slipped along from wall to wall, from one hiding place to another, like a commando on a raid. His big fear was that he might knock a stone from a wall and attract their attention.

There was danger of detection too from his binocular case and camera banging together as he skipped from place to place. "Jettison glasses," he told himself. He placed the binoculars on a prominent boulder that looked different from the rest. He would collect them on his way back.

When he looked around for the mother and child they had disappeared. He couldn't believe it, as if the ground had opened up and swallowed them. As he moved gingerly on he soon saw the reason. The roadway wound into a narrow pathway and descended fairly steeply between the rocks to a little beach. It had more likely been built for donkeys to draw seaweed than for tourists to go swimming. Johnson stopped to light a cigarette, then remembered the smell would travel on the fresh air, and quenched it again.

He edged forward slowly to the edge of the rock which overhung the little beach. The sight that greeted his eyes would have been an answer to prayer if he believed in prayer. Mother and child were gambolling naked in the water. "A great pair of knockers," he said to himself as he withdrew from the edge of the rockcliff to concentrate on preparing his camera. Leaning forward again, this time with camera in hand. He focused on somewhere around Teresa's navel to make sure both breasts and pubic hair were included in his shots as she tossed her little girl in the air and caught her again, letting her splash down into the water. The child was making such a din with her joyful shouts and laughter that there was no danger the clicking of the camera would be heard.

As Johnson hurried away he was already thinking of the headlines—"WHAT PRIEST IS DYING FOR," maybe. He knew well which paper would publish this story. The only disappointment in what for him was a perfect day was failing to find his binoculars. There were many erratics, granite boulders scattered here and there on the limestone crag. On which had he left the glasses? Did it matter? This story would earn the price of a hundred pairs of binoculars.

❧

For the first time in many years Cóilín a' Phortaigh chanced going in to Tigh Bheartla, the local pub, on his own. Bartley's father had barred him many years before, but the son had never complained, maybe because he used to be with the priest, or with Neddy, Bartley's best customer. He had had no problem accepting being barred. The owner of a pub could do what he liked in his own house as far as Cóilín was concerned. He was apprehensive as he pushed in the swing door. All Bartley, who was mopping the floor, said was—"I'll be with you in a minute, Cóilín."

"A big pint there, Bartley, if you please." Cóilín ordered.

"You're on the road early this morning."

"I suppose it is early. It's hard to know with that old mist."

"I forgot, Cóil, that the sun is your clock."

"It's not a bad clock either, except when there isn't any sun."

"Well, on my watch it's seven minutes after ten. You must have an awful thirst on you. I hardly had the door opened."

"I chewed a lot of *duileasc* coming down the road. The same *duileasc* can be a salty old devil when it comes to the thirst."

"Why wouldn't it be salty and it straight out of the sea? Good for you, but not as good as this stuff." Bartley placed a pint on the counter. "Drinks on the house," he said. "I like to do that when there is only one customer in. No one can ever say I didn't stand a drink for everyone in the house."

"Thanks Bartley, and may it not be long until you do it again. And may you be seven times better off this time next year."

"Drink it up and don't be talking about it. I'll be back when I have the floor finished. It gets very grubby in this damp weather."

"It's a grand soft day alright, but maybe it will clear up like yesterday."

"It might be soft, Cóilín, but you can't say it's grand." Bartley had the floor nearly finished. "Sure as long as the porter isn't soft, we can't complain."

"Where is everyone?" Cóilín had never gone into an empty pub before.

"Signing on. There'll be the full of the house in after a while. It depends on what time the guards come around to open the barrack. It's awful that grown men have to stand out in the rain for a couple of hours for a chance to sign on for a few pounds. The trouble is that the same couple of guards have to do a couple of other places as well."

"They'll have their tongues out with the thirst when they get here."

"I better have the kettle boiled. Every one of them will have a hot whiskey as soon as they get in the door. They'll turn to the pints of porter then."

"It's a grand drink all the same." Cóilín swirled what was left of his pint in the bottom of his glass. "But it's not as good as the porter that used to be in it long ago. It would take two pints now to be as good as one pint that time."

"You'll have another one in you before the crowd comes in." Bartley placed another pint on the counter in front of Cóilín. "That's alright," he said as the older man put his hand in his pocket and drew out a fistful of notes and coins.

"That's too much altogether, Bartley."

"Sure it takes two now to be as good as one pint of the old porter."

"When you look at it like that..." Cóilín gave a big toothless smile. "I'll be back, Bartley."

"I used to think the old man was hard on you in years gone bye. This might help to make up for it. Sure he was hard on us all."

"The Lord have mercy on him." Cóilín raised his cap and set it back further on his head, as he always did in respect for the dead. "Sure I suppose he thought he was doing the right thing. And maybe he was." He would not speak badly of those that were gone.

"Nobody should be barred unless they are troublesome."

"I think he thought I was a bit dirty coming in from the bog."

"He was stubborn man. When he got an idea in his head there was no changing it."

"Isn't it great the way things have changed over the years."

"That sort of thing has changed for the better anyway, Cóilín, even though you still hear many a one harking back to the good old days."

"Everyone has a pound now." Cóilín was fondling a battered pound note, opening it it, inspecting it. "We didn't have a penny in the old days." He showed the picture of the woman on the note to Bartley. "Isn't that a grand girl there, now."

"As nice a woman as you would see in a day's walk, Cóilín"

"A grand woman, but she does be gone from you in the morning." Cóilín laughed heartily at his own joke.

"She doesn't last long in this day and age, but I think that them new coins go even quicker than your woman used to disappear."

"Them deers is very fast runners. It's hard to keep up with them. Sure they're not pounds at all, just big pennies." Cóilín sat drinking quietly as the bar owner bustled about, wiping tables and counter, restocking shelves. It was Bartley that rekindled the conversation;

"There was a stout thirty or forty years ago they used to call "Double X" I used to hear my father and I still hear some of the men here talking about it. They say it was fierce strong stuff altogether."

"And the barrels were so big," Cóilín reminisced. "Between the weight of the barrel and that strong porter within it."

"I often heard it said, Cóilín, that you were the only man in the place that could lift one of them barrels up over your head."

"An odd one," Cóilín said modestly.

"Every one, from what I've heard. Is it true that when the circus came you lifted more than their strong man?"

"That was a weak strong man. Sure he was good for nothing."

"They say that he was good, but that you were better."

"Sure they wanted me to go with them at the time."

"And why didn't you?"

"Ah, I had no English. I never heard anything but the old language and me growing up."

"Maybe the circus crowd didn't have much English either. Weren't they from Hungary or somewhere over there in eastern Europe."

"There was nothing hungry about that crowd. They were grand rounded women, and divil the much clothes they used to have on them, Bartley." Cóilín gave a conspitorial giggle. "I used to be telling them that they would catch cold, but sure they didn't know what I was saying."

"You should have married one of them and gone with the circus. You would have the world walked by now."

"Ah, my mother was alive at the time, and I couldn't leave her. And there was a rotten smell off them old elephants. Worse than pigs or hens the smell of what they used to leave behind them."

"Circus Cóilín. Cóilín a' tSorcais, I suppose you would have been called around here," Bartley mused. "What a fine exotic life you could have had, travelling the world, married to one of them Hungarian girls."

"Them were fine round girls, Bartley," Cóilín pictured them in the ring, swinging on ropes, or standing, skimpily dressed, one-legged on the backs of horses, "but do you know, they were a bit narrow in the hind quarters."

"Not good breeding stock," Bartley laughed lightly. "Not much good if you wanted the full of a house of children, like."

"I suppose one of them would have been better than nothing."

"I'm sure she would..." Bartley thought of Cóilín's miserable conditions, comparing them in his mind to what he considered the glamorous world of the circus. But the man opposite seemed happy and contented with his life. Maybe it was himself that was dissatisfied, had itchy feet, the desire to see the world. His reverie was interrupted by a sudden rush of men through the door of the bar. "Three hots there quick, Bartley. For a September day, it's awful damp, miserable and cold."

"And three pints to chase it down." Dara Nóra was rubbing his hands together, as he went towards the fireplace, only to find there was nothing in the grate. Tomeen McNicholl eased off the trousers of his weatherproof suit. "Only for the oilers I'd be drenched to the skin. That mist is worse than a decent shower of rain." He sat up on a high stool beside Cóilín, and clapped him on the back with his big broad hand. "How's she cuttin' there, Cóilín, a mhac?" Cóilín winced from the sudden slap. "Take it easy, there, Tomeen."

"You're not the first Tomeen gave the clap to Cóilín, and you probably won't be the last." Dara Nóra was in good form, despite the cold, now being dissipated by the whiskey.

"Speaking of which," Neddy said. "Is there any word about Johnny McKay?"

"That's a lot of codswallop." Bartley had heard the rumour too.

"He's riddled with it alright." Tomeen assured him. "It's only a matter of time."

"I hope he lives to be a hundred, to confound the lot of ye." Bartley topped up the pints and placed them before them, before moving on to serve a few more men who sat around the nonexistent fire.

"What's wrong with Johnny McKay?" Cóilín asked.

"Nothing that you're likely to pick up," Neddy

assured him.

"Unless the sheep have it." Tomeen was the only one to laugh at his own attempt at a joke. There was a lot of respect locally for Cóilín.

"That would be more your style, Tomeen." Dara said bluntly. "Give a hot to Cóilín here," he called over to Bartley.

"Aren't you the lucky man to have the pension," Tomeen said to Cóilín. "You don't have to stand out there in the rain waiting for the guards, to sign for a few miserable pounds on a Tuesday morning."

"Only for the same miserable pounds, we wouldn't have anything," Neddy said, as he paid for the first round of hot whiskies.

"Isn't it an easy week's work too when you think of it," Bartley remarked. "Sign your name on a Tuesday morning and get your cheque at the end of the week. When you look at it like that you could call yourselves civil servants, getting paid by the government..."

"Go on. Say it..." Neddy could take being slagged off about the dole from another recipient, but not from a man reputed to be a half millionaire.

"Say what?" Bartley was wary. Neddy seldom got excited or angry.

"Getting paid to do nothing, you mean. Well I can tell you to your face, Bartley, there wouldn't be much going across that counter either way, except the money we get from the government, as you put it. That's the money that has made you a rich man."

"Me! Sure I'm only pulling the devil by the tail. If you saw the tax demand I got the last day. They could wipe me out."

"Sure myself and Cóilín and the boys are wiped out with the tax too. Aren't we lads." Neddy's anger subsided as quickly as it had risen. "Murdered with the tax, we are. We wouldn't mind having your problem at all, Bartley."

"Don't get me wrong, Neddy. I don't mind where the money comes in from..."

"As long as you're stacking it.?"

"That's it, now." Bartley hurried away to the other end of the counter, reminding himself to be more sensitive about things like the dole. It took a very small spark to set off a conflagration in a pub. It was many a long day since his father had told him that. He was lucky that it had happened in the morning, before they had much taken. Then again, at night when they would be well oiled they might have just made a joke of it. You couldn't be too careful.

"Anything new, Coilín?" Dara Nóra inquired.

"Devil the news."

"How is your mate today?"

"Father Pat?"

"Who else?"

"I haven't seen him yet, today. I was at the door earlier, but I didn't see anyone around. With the day so dull I didn't realise that it was so early." Cóilín suddenly spat out one of the cloves he had swallowed with the hot whiskey. "I don't like them ould horns in the drink."

"Horns?" Bartley was suddenly concerned. The last thing he wanted was a legal action.

"Them black old devils." Cóilín took another of them off his tongue, and with a disgusted look on his face, showed it to the barman.

"That's only a clove, Cóilín."

"I knew it had something to do with the devil." The others didn't know was he being serious or not.

"But they put a nice taste on the hot whiskey."

"Not as nice as that American whiskey Father Pat has." Cóilín remembered his last visit to the presbytery. "I wonder did he start to eat anything yet?"

"He'll need to start soon..." Bartley didn't need to finish his sentence. The bar was like a wakehouse for a few minutes, as if the priest had already died. When Neddy thought that the respectful silence had gone on for long enough, he remarked. "This damp old weather is a bitch for the arthritis." Feeling his right shoulder with his left hand he wound his right arm around in its socket.

"They say the change in the weather affects the arthritis and the rheumatism." Dara Nóra was glad to get away from discussing the priest's problem. He was fed up arguing with his son, Pádraig about it, and Aisling was as bad since she had her appendix out Reek Sunday. "The bones never gave me any trouble, myself, even though I worked and worked hard, in both this country and England."

"Of course it was the rifle gave me the arthritis." Neddy was still loosening out his shoulder. "Shooting at the huns and the japs with my trusty 303."

"It's the first I heard you mention about the Japanese." Bartley winked at the other men, across the counter."

"Sure, wasn't I everywhere. Dunkirk. Pearl Harbour. Yeepers. Korea. You name it. Neddy John Tom was in it."

"I understood that it was in England you joined the army." Tomeen was inclined to take things logically, even though he never noticed Neddy mixing his wars.

"It was in England I enlisted." Neddy had often

heard that you need a good memory to be a liar. It was getting harder and harder to extricate himself from the knots he tended to tie himself up in, but God had blessed him with a good imagination. He always thought of something. "It was in England I enlisted, alright," he repeated, "but it was the American army I joined, if you get me." No one looked as if they had got him. Neddy continued—"Naturally enough I had refused to join the British army until they gave us back the six counties."

"But what about this fellow Bert you were telling us about the last day?" Dara Nóra tried to deepen the hole Neddy had dug for himself, to see what kind of Houdini escape he would come up with this time. "If I remember Bert correctly, he had a distinct English accent."

"That's the point, Dara." Neddy didn't bat an eyelid. "I was seconded by the Americans to the British, to keep up morale, as it were. De Valera himself discussed it with Joe Kennedy, the American ambassador in London, and father of the late, great president, Jack." He knew that mention of two such icons would deflect further analysis of his wartime exploits. Not everyone present was as respectful, or certainly not for the same reasons. It was Tomeen who unintentionally brought the house down with laughter when he remarked. "Jack Kennedy was great alright, great in bed, they say, a great man for the ride."

"You never lost it, Tomeen..."

℧

Father Pat Barrett awoke suddenly. Martina McKay, in her school uniform, stood looking distraught, at the foot of his bed. "Martina?" He tried to raise himself from the pillows, but felt stiff, sore and weak.

"They think my daddy has AIDS." she blurted out, and began to cry uncontrollably, her body racked by great sobs.

"Sit down. Sit down, Martina." She sat gingerly on the edge of the bed. "Who says that your daddy had AIDS?"

"Aisling Dara Nóra…Everyone at school thinks it." Slowly and gradually the story came out, between tears and sobs. At lunchtime that day Martina had approached Aisling to try and find out what the boycott was about, why she especially was so aggressive and hurtful to her since the school was reopened.

"Get away from me, you bloody bitch," Aisling had screeched at her, drawing the attention of everyone in the school yard. Martina had tried to calm her down by saying quietly. "I didn't tell anyone about Croagh Patrick."

"That has nothing to do with it."

"What is it so?"

"You're fucking contaminated. That's what it is." Aisling spat her words at her.

"Contaminated?"

"Everyone knows what has your father in hospital."

"TB. TB isn't contagious. You can ask the doctor if you want."

"AIDS" She could still see Aisling's expression in her mind's eye, her eyes standing in her head, her mouth stretched wide as if held open with plastic tape, screeching "AIDS." Martina had run from the school, ran down the road, ran, ran, running to the sea, to drown herself, something, anything to take away the pain. She had eventually dropped, exhausted against a grassy bank by the side of the road. What was she to do? Her mother was to go to hospital that day to see her father. She had no one to talk too. She wished she had waited for Davoren. She hadn't even thought of Davoren. But she couldn't go back to the school. She was never going back to school. She would not be alive to go back to school. Then she saw the gable of the church from where she lay. There might be some comfort there. She dragged her feet after her. The running had worn her out.

She could not concentrate, could not pray when she went in to the church, but it did help to calm her down a little. Then she thought of Father Pat. How they missed him in the school. He would have been the one to go to, to sort out something like this. Why not go to him now? There was no one else. At least he would listen. If he were able.

He did listen. He knew, as he listened that he was definitely going to give up his hunger-strike. He had probably decided a long time ago, he thought, but it was Martina's problem that brought home to him the selfishness and arrogance of his own position. Here was someone who needed him, who did not need Pat Barrett, but needed a priest. Needed Pat Barrett, the priest might be more like it. Here I am, thinking of myself again, he thought, when Martina asked: "What am I going to do?"

"I don't believe your father has AIDS, Martina," he began. "But even if he has, I think you should love him and care for him. That is more important than what anyone thinks. In the same way I think that if you come home pregnant to him some day, he should love you and care for you. Not that I'm comparing pregnancy to AIDS." He stopped. "Would you do me a favour?"

"What favour?"

"Would you ready me a drop of soup? And then we'll do the talking. You talk, and I'll listen. You won't be expected at home until four o' clock? That should give plenty of time."

❧

Pat Barrett's news that he had come off his hunger-strike could not have come at a more opportune time for his bishop, Thomas Doherty. Eugene Johnson, the journalist was already in the waiting room beside what the bishop called his "inner sanctum." Anthony Cosgrave would have him well nicely oiled and glad-handled before the interview. One of the perks of his position was to let someone like Johnson stew outside for a while, while the bishop was busy. He reached for his breviary. It could have waited, but then Barrett's news had come like an answer to his persistent prayers. "My soul doth magnify the lord..." Doherty felt as if his spirits were soaring on the poetic words of the Magnificat.

Prayers finished, the bishop phoned the nuncio. He would need to be informed before Johnson got his scoop. McIntosh snorted with satisfaction. "Well done, Tom. I knew you would pull it off. Mein Papa will be very pleased."

"I'm sure mein Führer is pleased too," the bishop said, referring to the nuncio, but he did not say it until he had hung up the phone. "Quintessential cute hoor," he said, quoting a journalist from Mayo as he caught a glimpse of himself in the sideboard mirror, on his way to the door to admit the Eugene Johnson.

He liked it. The description fitted.

Pat Barrett's decision to quit his anticelibacy protest largely pulled the sting from Johnson's prepared article intended to lacerate him as naive, hypocritical and opportunistic. On the other hand he had a scoop on his hands, the first journalist to be informed of the decision, with ready made quotes from what he described as "the safe pair of hands at the epicentre of the storm, Bishop Thomas Doherty." His front-page story did not mention Teresa Carter. Legal advice that she "could take us to the cleaners," saw to that.

The pictures the journalist took the day he spent stalking Jennie and Teresa did not go to waste, however. One shot of the birds came out very well and was captioned with a typically alliterative flourish as "Highspeed hunt of hawk." The legal team saw no difficulty in using the picture of Jennie and Teresa gambolling at the beach, so long as they were not named. There is nothing to stop anyone taking a snapshot at a beach, they said. It was published in the holiday section above the caption "Burren del sol."

❧

After much tooing and froing between Sister Damien, and Sean Donlon from the secondary school on the one hand and the rapidly recovering Pat Barrett on the other, a school Mass of explanation and reconciliation was arranged to take place as soon as the priest would be fit enough to celebrate it. All the parents, teachers and pupils were invited and over three quarters turned up. Johnny McKay did one of the readings, Davoren another. A doctor specialising in the treatment of AIDS patients gave the sermon, gave what he described as the "facts of life and death" about AIDS, helping to clear up many misunderstandings and misapprehensions.

Martina, still smarting from her ordeal did not say the bidding prayer prepared for her by Sister Damien. She composed her own—"Lord protect us from the worst disease of all, the false rumour. Lord, hear us..."

❧

"Pathetic," was Teresa's comment when she read the letter from Pat which her mother had posted on to her flat in the city. Pathetic because it contained Bishop Doherty's suggestion that that could live together with the blessing, or at least the connivance of the church. "That part of my life is over," she said to herself as she bundled up the letter and put it on the blazing fire.

It was Jake who came across the "Burren del sol" picture on the newspaper wrapping his fish and chips. "Who does that remind me of?" he said with his impudent smile. Teresa looked at it, smiled and did not say anything. Sinéad raised her eyebrows and nodded her head approvingly. "So they are real?" Jake said.

"You'll never know."

❧❧❧